Falling from Grace

Falling

from

Grace

Ann
McNichols

WALKER & COMPANY
NEW YORK

First published in the United States of America in 2000
by Walker Publishing Company, Inc.

Published simultaneously in Canada
by Fitzhenry and Whiteside,
Markham, Ontario L3R 4T8

Library of Congress Cataloging-in-Publication Data

McNichols, Ann.
    Falling from grace / Ann McNichols.
        p. cm.
    Summary: In a small Arkansas town in the 1930s,
thirteen-year-old Cassie Hill's grief-stricken sister
leaves town, her father becomes overly friendly with
the new preacher's wife, and her Sunday School
teacher causes trouble, but Cassie finds comfort in
her new friendship with a quiet boy from Hungary.
    ISBN 0-8027-8750-9
    [1. Interpersonal relations—Fiction.   2. Friendship—
Fiction.   3. Brothers and sisters—Fiction.   4. Family
life—Arkansas—Fiction.   5. Schools—Fiction.
6. Arkansas—Fiction.]   I. Title.
PZ7.M2365 Fal 2000
[Fic]
                                                    00-034955

Book design by Jennifer Ann Daddio

Printed in the United States of America

2 4 6 8 10 9 7 5 3 1

One

My sister, Adra, picked a good day to leave—Sunday. I hate Sundays. Sunday weighs on a person like a heavy coat in March. I don't blame her one bit for leaving. People in town stare at her and whisper ever since that boy she was seeing got himself killed by a train on purpose. People act like it was her fault. After it happened Adra acted mad at everyone and couldn't seem to abide Daddy telling her what to do. I am the only one who knows she took the train early this morning before anyone woke up. Even though we live a ways from the railroad tracks, you can hear the train whistle and the rumbling of the trains going by at night. Mostly I sleep through it, except this morning I knew that train was taking Adra off somewhere.

The smell of sausage cooking drifts upstairs, and I

know I'd better go help Mama with breakfast, even though I wish I were on the train with Adra.

The minute I get downstairs, Daddy tells me, "Go wake up your sister. She should be helping your mother." His eyes never leave the newspaper.

There is nothing for it but to go, though I do not want to go upstairs to Adra's room. The stairs are slick wood and feel cool, but I climb as if I'm walking up a steep hill barefoot, careful of jagged rocks, and slow as in the noonday sun.

Mama calls me back. "Leave Adra be. She hasn't been sleeping well. She can stay home this morning. Besides, Cassie is all the help I need," Mama says, which is fortunate, since I am all the help she is going to get. Jake and Tom think meals come ready to be set on the table.

I set the table with seven places, as if Adra had not gone, and then get the biscuits out of the oven. Jake, who's fourteen and getting taller every day, comes tearing down the stairs now that all the work of fixing breakfast has been done, slowing down as he reaches the table so as not to get a lecture from Daddy. Tom, who's already grown, takes a place next to Daddy and picks up the part of the paper Daddy isn't reading. They will read until Mama sits down.

After breakfast Mama wields the comb, choice instrument of torture. "Cassie, we have to do something with your hair. It's a mess of tangles. A bird could make a nest, and you'd never know it."

"I'd like that." I think how I'd tame baby birds, let them fly from the top of my head, birdsong in my ears, feathers around my steps.

"No, you wouldn't. Here, hold still." Mama rakes the comb down my neck. Sometimes Mama is patient with the comb, working through the tangles, but on Sunday morning she hurries. She says if we are not careful we will have a reputation for always being late for church, and once you have a reputation there is nothing you can do to change it.

Mama ties ribbons in my hair, scooping up sections and pulling them tight. They won't hold, though, even if I were to keep still like I am supposed to.

"That looks real nice, Cassie. Just try and be still."

Jake scrambles downstairs and pulls my hair before I can duck. One of the ribbons slides right out of my hair, and I pocket it before Mama can work me over anymore.

Tom doesn't go with us to church but drives us there and back because Daddy doesn't like to drive. Tom is happy to drive, for then he can use the car and go wherever he pleases the entire morning. Mama says Tom is grown and can make his own decisions. I can't wait until I am as old as Tom. Then they can't make me go to Sunday school ever again, or do anything else for that matter. Grown-ups always think they can tell children what to do, since they are smaller; can say, "Run fetch," and children are expected to mind. I can understand how Adra must have felt—here she is grown-up size, as big as she's going to grow, and Daddy acts as if she hasn't grown up at all.

Tom pulls the car, a 1926 Model T Ford, up by the porch and honks, unnecessarily because we are all in motion, Mama herding us out the door with Daddy following at a snail's pace, the last one to get in the car, where he rides next to Tom. Tom drives sedately, as if the desire to go fast has never crossed his mind. Daddy will have trouble holding Jake back when he is old enough to drive. Mama doesn't drive and has no desire to. Daddy says women don't need to drive, says there's no need for women to be out gallivanting around the country when there's plenty to keep busy at home. Mama has never taken exception to this line of thought, but I have a plan that will get Mama to drive and open the way for me. I plan to give Mrs. Edwards, the preacher's wife, the notion to drive by showing her an advertisement of a pretty lady driving a car. When Mrs. Edwards sees it is Style, she will not balk but will scoot poor Preacher Edwards right out of the driver's seat. Mama is not one to be outshone, especially by someone like Mrs. Edwards, who has caused some astonishment already by coming to church wearing the brightest red lipstick you ever saw. I heard some of the ladies say it is a color called crimson, and Mrs. Cranby, my Sunday school teacher, said it is sinful to wear lipstick at all. Since Mrs. Edwards started wearing the crimson lipstick to church, other ladies have started wearing lipstick, not crimson, but paler shades. Since Mrs. Edwards is so colorful, Preacher Edwards does not give sermons about wearing cosmetics or talk about painted ladies the way the preacher before him did, so that none of the ladies dared wear the makeup they bought down at the drugstore.

If the preacher's wife takes to driving, Daddy is likely to buy Mama her own car. Daddy is proud to have risen in the world, becoming a banker, instead of a preacher like he was supposed to. Since his daddy was a preacher, Daddy grew up wearing clothes donated by the congregation and insists Mama buy firsthand. Daddy says things like, "clothes make the man," as if you might be changed somehow by wearing nice clothes. Marylou, this girl in my class, wears pink ruffles to Sunday school and looks like a candy cane, and she's mean as a snake. Well, snakes aren't mean exactly, just naturally defensive, like you'd be if someone like Jake had hold of your tail and swung you in a wide circle, then let go to see if your tail'd come off. Jake is likely to join up with an outlaw gang when he's old enough, where he will fit right in, though Daddy thinks Jake might be the moon and the stars and for his last birthday gave him a shotgun, which should be a great help establishing his outlaw career.

It is not a long way from our house to the Baptist Church. The town we live in, Prosper, Arkansas, has 905 residents according to the sign as you come into town, and I can walk from one end to the other in no time at all. Tom pulls up near the church and opens Mama's door, helping her out and then turning to help me out. He says, "Where's the sunshine gone, kid? Don't let them get you down."

Tom cannot begin to understand a fraction of the torture that belongs to me on Sunday mornings. He does not have to go to the thirteen-year-old girls' Bible class taught by Mrs. Cranby, where I have not one friend. I wish I could go to church up on the mountain, instead of here. They speak in tongues, and Daddy says they act like heathens, and that religion is a loose term for what goes on in their meetings. I have heard sometimes they handle snakes, and one day I'll just have to go and see. Maybe it would be like Moses turning his rod into a snake to scare those Egyptians. I wish I could turn a rod into a snake during Sunday school class, or better yet during the sermon, when the everlasting drone puts the entire congregation to sleep and the only bright spot is Mrs. Edwards's crimson lipstick.

All six girls in my class shift closer to each other, their petticoats rustling like the sound the wind makes in the trees. I take the chair by the window, a little away from the group. Lizzie, who was my friend until last summer, whispers to Marylou, and I hear my name but nothing else. Lizzie and I used to play games where we pretended we were characters in books. One day last summer she told me she was too old for imaginary games, and when I suggested we go berry picking, she sniffed and said there were too many chiggers in the woods to suit her. Since then she prefers to talk to Marylou about boys and seems to have forgotten we were ever friends.

I wonder if I forgot to clean my fingernails. No, it's my gloves I forgot. All six are wearing white gloves, like they are members of some club.

I can feel the remaining ribbons in my hair already coming loose from when I leaned out the window to feel the wind better. I sit down, Daddy's old Bible in my lap. I like the feel of the soft leather. It belonged to Daddy when he was a boy and is mine now. Neither Tom nor Jake wanted it. During church I read the passages he's marked to pass the time while the rest of the girls my age sit on the back pew and giggle. I wish Adra would have stayed. I could sit with her. Adra always looks elegant, and she has this smile that says she knows everything there is to know.

Mrs. Cranby finally makes an appearance, huffing up the stairs and entering the narrow door sideways, not exactly a grand entrance but a real achievement for someone her size. I've heard Mama say Mrs. Cranby was a skinny little thing years ago when they were in school together. Mrs. Cranby fans herself, although it is not hot.

"Girls, come to order. Marylou, will you lead us in prayer?" Mrs. Cranby says when she gets her breath. Mrs.

Cranby likes Marylou, who pretends to be interested in the lessons. I believe I drive her crazy asking questions whenever I don't understand something. Grown-ups do not like to spend their time trying to figure out answers and expect you to take them at their word.

Marylou smirks and begins, "Thank you, Jesus, for this day and for our church and especially for Mrs. Cranby who comes to teach us. Amen."

I let myself drift away, watching a flock of birds circling above the tall pines just out the window until they settle in the trees. If I could fly, I would just keep going on into the distant blue.

Then I notice they are all looking at me as if they expect me to say something.

"Cassie," Mrs. Cranby says, folding her arms across her chest, "most of us come here to learn about God's word. You have not been paying attention."

Lizzie murmurs, "And who in their right mind would?" and for a second it seems as if Lizzie might be sorry I am caught daydreaming, but then Marylou whispers, a constant humming like the buzz of a fly, reclaiming Lizzie.

Mrs. Cranby turns a slit-eyed look at Lizzie, as if momentarily distracted, but she comes right back to me and says, "Cassie, we have been learning about Adam and Eve and how sin came into the Garden of Eden."

I relax. I already know this story.

Mrs. Cranby holds her fan poised in the air and asks, "Who brought sin into the Garden of Eden? Cassie, you may answer."

"God," I answer, "since God planted the tree in the garden when he must have known exactly what would happen."

Mrs. Cranby fans the air furiously. "You know very well the serpent tempted Eve, and Eve persuaded Adam to disobey."

"I know, but—"

"There are no buts, there is only what the Bible tells us. Who do you think you are to make up your own answers?"

Lizzie is the only one who doesn't look at me like I'm a blasphemer. She has this expression of interest that shows she is considering possibilities. Lizzie used to like to figure things out for herself and not just take everything as fact. Marylou whispers loud so I can hear her say to Lizzie, "Cassie thinks she's so smart," and Lizzie whispers something to Marylou, so I know I've lost her.

Marylou has never liked me. I used to think it was because Lizzie liked me better than her. Now she has Lizzie all to herself, you'd think she'd leave me alone. I don't know what comes over me, but the next thing I know I am aiming a kick at the frilly pink ruffle that is Marylou's behind, a prime target, and softer than a football. Marylou falls forward out of her chair, and for a second I worry I kicked her too hard, but she gets right up and slaps me.

"Cassie, you are the worst behavior problem in this class." Mrs. Cranby pulls me up by my collar as if I'm likely to run away and acts like Marylou is totally innocent. Mrs. Cranby's face is almost purple, and I wonder if she will sit on me and squash me, as surely she could.

She says, "You will sit in the hall for the rest of the lesson. We will pray for you."

Marylou smirks, the ultimate satisfaction of triumph shining from her eyes. She beams like polished silver.

Voices fill the hallway from the classrooms, all running together, and after a while I close my eyes. I don't hear him come up behind me, folding his fingers over my eyes.

"Guess who?"

I don't have to guess. I know it's Jake.

"Leave me alone. I'm in enough trouble already."

"How did you know it was me?" Jake asks, bouncing from one foot to another.

"Why aren't you in class?" I ask.

"I slipped out while they were praying."

"Jake, you are up to something." Jake's mouth is a dead giveaway—it twitches like a rabbit's.

Jake pulls something from his pocket and opens his hand like it's a gift.

"Food coloring? What are you going to do with it?"

"Promise to keep it to yourself, and I'll let you help."

"All right."

There is only one place in church that contains water—

the baptistery. It is at the front of the church behind a curtain. It is like an enormous bathtub, large enough for two people to stand up, the water coming up to their chests. Behind it is a picture of river and trees, so that it gives the illusion that the person being baptized is outside in a river, just the way John baptized Jesus. If Jake dyes the water with blue food coloring, the people who are baptized, who will think the water is natural blue, will go under and come out sputtering, cleansed of sins that may be scarlet, but anyone who stays in for more than a minute will be at least a robin's-egg blue. Preacher Edwards, who will remain in the water the longest, will be the bluest color of all, and finally more noticeable than his colorful wife.

"Cassie, if you want to help, stop daydreaming and come on." It's a generous offer, and I tread my way down the hall after Jake.

We slip past the slow, sleepy voices where the women's Bible class meets. The door is open, but their backs are to us. We slip past the older girls' class, where they talk in raised voices as if there is something exciting going on. Outside the window we can see the old men gathered under a tree. They don't go to class at all, just smoke and talk in the shade of the trees. There's a stairway that takes us to the front of the church, and we slip into a room behind the pulpit that is curtained off from the auditorium. Jake hands me a small glass vial, such a dark blue it looks almost black, and says, "You can be first, if you want to."

I can't believe how gentlemanly Jake is behaving. I wonder vaguely how sacrilegious dying water is, whether the water is holy somehow, if it will reject the dye. The color swirls and melts away so that you can't see it at all. Jake opens another vial and dumps it efficiently, and then adds another. His pockets are full of vials of dye, all blue. The tub is constructed of blue tiles so the color of the water becomes all the more blue, but not noticeable, just maybe a deeper blue than before. I run my finger through the water, swirling it, and it comes out with a faint tinge.

"I should have bought more dye. I've only a few vials left," Jake says. Jake is a perfectionist. He muses, "I calculated the cubic feet and came out with five hundred gallons. It should work exactly. I don't know why it's not darker. Maybe if you leave your finger in longer it will hold the dye."

"Shhhh. Someone's coming." I hear voices in the room next to us, a storage room where they keep extra hymnals and the nativity display they put up every Christmas.

I stand by the curtain keeping watch while Jake empties the rest of the dye.

"I missed seeing you this week." It's a woman's voice.

"You know I have responsibilities, a family."

I'd know that voice anywhere. Daddy is talking to some lady, telling her about his responsibilities—us.

"I'd never thought I'd miss seeing you. You weren't there on Wednesday afternoon," she says.

Now Daddy is calling some woman, not Mama, darling. I pull the curtain just enough so I can see Daddy holding Mrs. Edwards, the preacher's wife. I hold my breath like I am in a vacuum, and the silence frames a longing for the moment before the awful knowing. I wonder if Eve felt like this after she took a bite of that apple, if she wished she could just spit it out as if she didn't like the taste, if maybe she saw the light fade, the colors of paradise diminishing, as if the world changed and became less new. I breathe finally, though I think I will never like the robin's-egg-blue shade my finger is. Outside is the glare of light, and the voices of the old men coming into the church, flicking away their cigarettes into the dirt.

Jake has finished emptying the vials. When Jake is involved in a project, he concentrates so hard he never notices anything around him. I don't think he heard them talking in the next room. He generally never pays much attention to anything Daddy says anyway.

Jake motions to me, whispering, "Cassie, let's go before someone catches us."

Outside people are visiting after Sunday school before going inside the church to settle on the long pews. Preacher Edwards catches me before I can get away.

"Cassie," he says, "Mrs. Cranby has been threatening to quit teaching the girls' class. Do you think you could help me out a bit? I'd hate for her to feel so bad she'd quit."

Preacher Edwards has taken me by surprise. He is very

tall and thin in his dark suit, but he leans back against the building while he is talking to me, so he doesn't stand up to his full height.

"I guess," I answer, wondering if this is a new kind of trouble.

"Well, I told her I'd have a talk with you and we'd get this straightened out. Will you try and get along with the other girls?"

"I can't promise I'll get along."

"But you'll try."

"I guess so." It is a topsy-turvy day. I am in trouble, and instead of outright saying so, Preacher Edwards is asking for my help as if I might be grown up. He is stooping, so he is not bending over me, and his face is so cheerful and kind, I hope he will never become consumed with an awful knowing.

Before I go into church I tear up the advertisement I intended to show Mrs. Edwards, the advertisement of the lady with style driving a car. I let the pieces fall into the grass. I find Mama and Daddy on the same pew they always sit on and slide in next to Mama. I don't dare to look at Daddy. Mama's face is reposeful, as if she is certain of things, but it is hard to guess what she is thinking.

Church follows the same pattern as always—hymns, announcements, prayers for the sick, and a long sleepy sermon, full of words that make me think of things other than church, words I catch and follow with a loose part of my mind, like chasing a butterfly, but not really wanting to catch it. Finally the time comes for Preacher Edwards to baptize new converts (we don't get many), people who rededicate their lives (a good revival can generate a multitude of these) and kids who are old enough. Jake is on the edge of the pew, waiting, like a scientist who wants to see the outcome of his experiment.

Preacher Edwards steps into the water first to read some Bible verses and set a solemn mood. He wears a white flowing robe, and he reaches his hand out to draw in the first person, and I am surprised to see Marylou. She is wearing a white robe over her pink dress, and I am torn between wicked pleasure and an almost sorrow, which makes no sense at all. Still, I watch the preacher duck her into the water and wonder if her pink skirt is becoming purple from the blue dye. There is no sign she has noticed as she steps out of the water, but before the next person is drawn into the water, an angry scream bursts out and echoes through the church. Marylou must have seen her blue toes and legs. The feeling of sorrow fades completely, and I catch Jake's gleaming eye, though his expression gives nothing away.

Preacher Edwards goes on as if there is nothing wrong. Mr. Mickey, who is next, is a regular for the baptismal process. Mr. Mickey is a near relation, being my aunt Opal's brother, and he sometimes goes for days without taking a bath or shaving or doing much else. He is not likely to notice or care if he is slightly blue. Everyone will shake his hand after church, though they know salvation will wear off eventually, just like the blue dye will wear off.

When the service finally comes to an end, people drift from the church, shaking their heads as if waking up in the noon sunlight. Marylou swishes out, having changed her wet dress, and is carrying on like she is the only person in the world who has ever suffered. She tells anyone who will listen how the water in the baptistery has been tampered with and the color has ruined her dress and maybe her whole life. People are polite, so they listen while thinking about fixing dinner or whatever else they have to do when they get home, nodding their heads as if they understand. I can see Daddy shaking hands with old Mrs. Betts and nodding his head as if Mrs. Betts is saying something altogether earthshaking, something he couldn't hear anyplace else. All the ladies, both young and old, like to talk to my daddy at church. I don't think it is only because he's nice looking. I think it's that he gives them his full attention, and doesn't look like he'd rather be off somewhere else. I look down the road to see if Tom is coming when Daddy calls me to come over to say hello to Mrs. Betts. She knew Daddy when he was a boy, but she won't tell me any stories about things he did then. I think she does not particularly like children. I don't want to go, but with social matters sometimes you do not have a choice. She reaches to grab my hand before I can resist and doesn't shake it but clutches it as if otherwise I might run off.

"Cassie, you are becoming a fine young lady."

Daddy gives me a look that says, Mind your manners.

"Thank you," I say, trying to pry my hand free of her grip. Then I notice she has hold of my blue-fingered hand, and Daddy is looking right at my blue-stained finger.

Daddy will not have missed the way Marylou carried on about her dress as she came out of church, and likely his banker's mind is busy calculating how I am involved.

Mrs. Betts still has hold of my hand. She says, "Cassie, you must stop by and see me after school one day."

"All right," I say, all the while wishing she'd let go of my hand.

Finally she drops my hand and goes on talking with Daddy, who has the beginning of a frown growing above his eyes where his brows come together as if he has weighed the possibilities and is unhappy with the outcome. He must have remembered he and Mrs. Edwards were in the next room to the baptistery, and he is wondering whether I was dyeing the water at the same time. I look away and clasp my hands behind my back, as if I could so easily hide away secrets.

Daddy continues talking to Mrs. Betts like there is nothing wrong. I hear him telling her how well she looks and how he'll send me or Jake over to run errands one day next week, and to let him know if she needs anything at all.

Jake strolls up, his hands in his now-empty pockets. He says, "So, what do you think? Not too bad for a Sunday morning."

I shrug. I'd rather not think at all, ever. Things are changing all around me, and I feel like I am being blown by a strong wind in a direction I did not choose to go. I wish I were like Adra, gone off to seek my fortune out in the world.

Everyone is getting into their cars to go home when Preacher Edwards comes out of the church with his wife. Since he wears a dark suit, you can't see even a hint of the blue shade that must cover him.

Two

On the way home Mama says, "Did you notice Mr. Mickey's color today?"

A glimmer of a smile surfaces on Jake's face and is eclipsed. Jake wears the mask of the good outlaw, not giving away a thing, as he lounges against the seat cushion, fearful of nothing on earth.

Daddy answers, "Normally I'd say Mr. Mickey's looking poorly could be attributed to his deplorable life, but that is not the case today. Didn't you hear the Browns' little girl carrying on about someone dyeing the water in the baptistery? I'm surprised you missed it."

"Oh," Mama says, "I hadn't realized I had missed anything."

Tom laughs. "Someone dyed the water in the baptistery? I wish I'd thought of it."

Furrow lines plow an old row on Daddy's brow, and Tom coughs, deflecting further laughter. "Years ago," Tom adds, "when I was younger. Certainly not now."

"Had you done so, you'd have been whipped soundly."

One of the vials that held the dye is still in my pocket, and I close my fingers over the glass and hold it so tight it is liable to break. I wonder what Jake has done with the empty vials, though he wears the look of the satisfied criminal who has disposed of the evidence.

"I wish I'd been in church today," Tom says.

"I am glad to hear you say so. Perhaps you'll come with us next Sunday," Daddy says.

"That would be real nice, Tom, if you would. I miss having you along," Mama says, touching Tom's shoulder. No one in my family touches each other much. I never see Daddy holding Mama the way he had his arms around Mrs. Edwards. I wonder what Mama is thinking, if she wishes Tom were with her at church for comfort the way I wished I had Adra next to me.

Of course, Adra is grown up, but she still does things a kid would do, like one day when we walked up the mountain and found a family of foxes. Adra was wearing a pair of Tom's overalls, even though Daddy disapproves of women wearing pants. She curled her long hair up under Tom's hat, so anybody who'd see her would think it was

Tom. They both have high cheekbones, which come from my great-grandmother, who was part Cherokee. Daddy has Cherokee blood, but he doesn't acknowledge it. Sometimes I wonder about my great-grandmother, who died before I was born. I guess she had to walk on that trail all the way from North Carolina to Oklahoma when she was my age. Her people moved from Oklahoma across the border to Arkansas to farm when she was older, and that's when she met my great-grandfather. Adra was walking quiet like Indians do in books you read, gliding like a dancer over patches of leaves and twigs. When we reached the rock at the top, she leaned over the edge, not one bit afraid of falling. Adra had never been afraid of anything, but after Ben's death she has changed, as if she knew something so sad she couldn't tell anyone. That day she seemed to forget.

You could see the whole valley below. There was a glow where the sun shone on the red maple leaves, which littered the copper-colored earth. You'd think the earth was storing sunlight, holding it for when the world turns dark. We were lying on the rock when we saw them come traipsing out of the woods into the clearing below. The mother sniffed the air, but the wind was blowing the wrong way for her to catch our scent. She began to lick their fur, and after a few minutes, like small children who don't like to sit still, the puppies pulled away and darted around her. Every now and then she'd snap at one, nipping gently as if reminding them to mind their manners. We watched without talking, and it was not until after they disappeared back into the trees that Adra spoke.

"They are beautiful."

"I wish I could tame one and take it home," I said.

"You can't tame wild things. It wouldn't be right."

I know this as well as Adra, but still I thought next time I will bring some food for the mother, who is real skinny so her bones show. Maybe they will come close if I bring food.

"They must live in a cave over in those rocks. We can't tell anyone," I told Adra, even though it is not likely she would mention it to Jake. Jake has taken to carrying that shotgun off in the woods. He killed a rabbit last week. He makes me mad, the way he shoots things, though I know this is what boys do.

"Our secret." Adra smiled. "We'd better get back before supper." Adra slipped off through the woods like a wild creature, her long hair falling out from under her hat, the same color as the foxes' coats, and as she glided ahead I was reminded of how the foxes blended into the woods and slipped away.

Mama is going to be upset Adra is gone, but she has Tom, and she depends on Tom, more than the rest of us. It is hard to know what she thinks, since like Jake she keeps her feelings inside and does not allow her face to be read like some library book anybody can check out. To read Mama, you have to know the secret code, indecipherable except with study and practice. Daddy has had both and says, "Tom, you are free to come and go as you like, but it would make your mother happy if you would accompany us next Sunday."

Tom sighs.

The sudden focus on Tom allows Jake to unleash the smile which he has buried, no longer wearing his secretive outlaw mask.

I will never be an outlaw, not a good one anyway. Words Preacher Edwards says time and again run through my mind—"For all have sinned and come short of the glory of God"—and it is as if the glory of God is a luminous rainbow that ends abruptly, just fades into the sky instead of reaching the earth. Glory has gone someplace else, like Adra has. I wish I could turn my blood to iron or some metal that is hard and cold, and then I wouldn't feel so empty.

Tom changes the subject and begins talking about expanding the store he runs for Daddy. Daddy is both a banker and store owner. Tom could have gone to work either place, but he chose the store. I'd choose the same. Some days I stop at the store, and Tom lets me ring up purchases with the big cash register. Everybody talks to you. At the bank it's real quiet, almost like being in church. I guess people wouldn't leave their money in a place where people were having a good time, like Tom has when he rides me around on the cart he uses to unload things, or sometimes, when business is slow, handwrites a sign that says, "If you need anything, come and get me at the drugstore." We go there and drink Coca-Cola in tall glasses. Of course, Tom is all business the days Daddy is coming to the store. One thing about Daddy is, he always lets Tom know when he's coming.

Tom says, "The country is becoming more prosperous. You have to think big."

"Not too big. You have to weigh every consideration. How much people around here can afford to buy. You stock according to need; otherwise you won't be able to move your merchandise."

Tom lets Daddy talk, but I bet he is already figuring how to get around Daddy and stock the shelves with things people don't need, but might develop an interest in if they had the opportunity.

First thing when we get home, Mama goes upstairs to Adra's room. She stands at the top of the stairs as if she has forgotten something important, holding her hat in her hand and winding it around her fingers in a circular motion.

"Adra's gone," Mama says, her voice all hollow as if it is an echo of itself. She has the note Adra wrote to say good-bye.

Daddy bounds upstairs and reads the note, then cracks his paper against the banister. "Damnation. Adra's been nothing but trouble. . . . I don't want to hear another word about Adra. She's no longer a member of this family," Daddy says in a tight voice. He stands on the stairs a moment, then comes back downstairs and goes into the parlor, where he sits in his favorite chair by the window.

Mama goes into Adra's room and closes the door. Tom looks as if he cannot make up his mind whether to go upstairs to comfort Mama or stay downstairs to talk to Daddy. After a minute he climbs the stairs and knocks on Adra's door.

Jake looks like there is a whirlwind inside him, and I can tell he can't stand another minute in the house. He breaks out the door and is gone. I don't know what to do with myself. I feel all torn up inside, like I am in pieces that don't fit back together. Maybe I should have told Mama about Adra going, only I know that would have been wrong. I don't figure they will ever know I knew, but I still feel terrible. I roam the yard outside and find my yellow cat, General Robert E. Lee. He listens to anything I say and licks himself all the while as comfortable as anyone could be, as if there isn't really anything more important in the world than to lick himself clean and to lie in the sunshine.

———

Later Tom comes out. "Cassie, I don't think Mama's going to fix dinner. She's lying down. Where's Jake?"

"He took off."

"Well, why don't you make yourself a sandwich and come riding with me? I'm driving up on the mountain."

Any other time I'd jump at the chance to go with Tom, but today feels like it will last and last and there's nothing I can do that will make any difference.

"Don't worry, kiddo. Adra is perfectly capable of taking care of herself. Don't mind what Daddy says. He'll get over it."

"I'm not worried."

"You could have fooled me."

I don't want Tom guessing at my thoughts, so I ask about Lula, this girl he likes who lives up on the mountain.

"Are you and Lula going to get married?"

"I'm just waiting for her to make up her mind."

"Well, tell her to hurry up." I like Lula. She's not glamorous like Mrs. Edwards. One day I saw Tom and Lula in the woods, when they didn't see me. I wasn't trying to spy, but they passed below the tree where I was sitting. If I'd have said anything, it would be like breaking a spell. Tom had woven flowers in a chain and put them in her hair, and even though she was wearing a faded cotton dress, she looked like a fairy-tale princess.

Tom drives absently, one hand on the wheel. He says,

"Lula's little sister, Nan, has been after me to bring you to visit."

I've seen Lula's sister before, but I don't really know her. When we arrive at Lula's, Tom pulls into the yard, where a swarm of little boys climb all over the car and then jump on Tom, clinging to his neck. Tom carries the littlest one on his shoulders, and the others follow us up to the house. Nan is on the porch steps waiting for us. She is not as tall as me, but her hair is longer than mine and braided in two thick braids. Lula is on the swing and doesn't get up to greet Tom, just smiles this long smile.

Nan says, "Come with me. Do you like baby calves? We have one."

Nan, barefoot though summer is over and the leaves have turned, leads the way to the barn, dark and warm and smelling like fresh hay and milk and warm animals. Nan climbs over the fence into the stall.

From the fence I stroke the calf's satin-soft neck. He watches us with deep eyes and catches Nan's sleeve with his mouth, lifting her arm and pulling on her sleeve as if trying to suck.

"Where's his mother?"

"She's in the field right outside. She won't go far away from him."

Nan notices right away my finger has traces of the blue dye and says, "Why is your finger blue?"

"We were dyeing something."

Nan climbs up on the stall fence and perches beside me. She says, "I have an idea. I can dye my finger blue, and we can have a special club."

I hate clubs more than anything.

Nan says, "You can be president. We'll let my little brothers join, so we can have lots of members."

"Okay," I answer. Maybe because Nan lives out in the country she doesn't know clubs are generally exclusive about their membership. Daddy is a Mason, and they don't just let anybody that wants to join. Adra told me about sororities at college, which sounds a lot like this club Marylou and Lizzie started after school, and I wouldn't join even if they asked. Nan is off to pump a bucket of water, and then we go into the kitchen to look for dye. She can't find any, then I remember the vial still in my pocket, which has a few drops of color left. I give it to Nan, who seems as pleased as Jake was earlier today. She drops the drops into the water, mumbling a chant she is making up on the spot: "Water clear, water blue, now and forever hold us true." Nan swirls her finger into the water for a minute, closing her eyes, as if it is a spell she is casting. Then she raises her finger in the air to dry it, admiring her work.

Nan places her finger against mine and says, "We match. I'll call the boys."

They come running and are delighted to join our club. Nan finds a blindfold and turns them in a circle, and then she dyes each of their fingers. She tells them on pain of death they must never tell the secrets of the club, although we have not made up any secrets yet.

Later we go into the kitchen to make lemonade. Tom and Lula are still out on the porch, and Lula is laughing at something Tom said, her voice musical as soft bells.

Nan says, "They just sit for hours and hours. I can't imagine why anyone wants to court. They sit out there like old people."

Nan's mother comes in where we are making lemonade and says, "Hi, Cassie. I'm so glad you could come up and see us. Why don't you all take a glass out to your sister and Tom. They would appreciate it."

"I'm sure," Nan giggles, "they have been working so hard pushing that swing back and forth."

"Nan, what's gotten into you, making fun of your sister." She notices Nan's blue finger. "What on earth have you been into?"

"Nothing," Nan says, rolling her eyes skyward.

We take the glasses out on the porch. Tom has an arm around Lula's shoulder and takes a glass of lemonade with his other hand. He hands one to Lula before taking one for himself.

He says, "Thank you. You girls been having fun?" Then, noticing Nan's blue finger, which is like mine, he says, "Is this some kind of conspiracy?" Tom has this reflective look on his face, and his brows grow together the way Daddy's do, only Tom's brows are not bushy and Tom never looks angry. He says, "So, Cassie, I see you found some way to entertain yourself at church. You are the quiet one."

Nan and I wander away from the porch, and Nan says, "Your brother doesn't talk like folks up here. What does conspiracy mean?"

The only conspiracy I can think of is in *Julius Caesar*, this play both Tom and Adra read in school, and which I read along with them mostly to be sociable so I could understand what they were talking about. The conspirators form a secret group so they can gang up on Caesar.

"A conspiracy is a bunch of people plotting against someone."

Nan sweeps her toe in the dirt before she says, "Let's be conspirators and plot to get your brother to marry my sister, and then we can be like sisters."

"Won't you miss Lula if she gets married and moves away?"

"She can be real bothersome. She has to have everything just so. I used some of her hair ribbons for the animals, playing county fair, and she screamed bloody murder. Of course, I should have asked her, but she would have just said no."

"Well, what if she'd have taken your ribbons?"

"Couldn't have. I've lost all mine." Nan twirls across the yard in a dance she is making up.

My eyes open wider, and I stare at Nan as if I'm seeing her for the first time. Here is someone like me. If I were going to tell anyone, maybe I could tell Nan, but there are some things you will never tell anyone, not even someone who might understand.

Some things do not bear telling. Some things you carry close and don't let go, as if by burying it inside it will not be so. I can still imagine Daddy kissing Mrs. Edwards on her crimson lips. Mama never wears lipstick as bright as Mrs. Edwards's. Maybe Daddy is drawn by that brightness. When I grow up, I will never wear lipstick nor kiss anyone. The thought of kissing a boy makes me gag. I don't know why my mind is all filled up with the sight of Daddy kissing and folding his arms around Mrs. Edwards, careful, as if she were made of glass.

"Cassie, you aren't listening."

"Sorry, I guess I was thinking."

"What about?"

"Nothing, it doesn't matter."

"Well, stop thinking, then. You don't look happy when you think. Let's get Bud and go exploring."

I wonder who Bud is, but don't have to wait long to find out. Bud is a spotted dog with floppy ears, who lies in the cool dirt and doesn't much want to go with us. Nan ties a lead on him and pulls him up. When we reach the woods, he comes alive and pulls on the lead as he catches a scent of something. Nan is almost flying down the trail trying to hold on to the rope. All of a sudden Bud comes to a stop, and his whole back end quivers, his tail jutting out like an iron rod.

"He's found birds. I'll let him loose, and we can watch them fly up all around."

When Nan unleashes Bud, he holds steady until she says, "Okay, go get them." Then Bud flings his whole body into a thicket, and you can hear the whir of wings around us as they fly upward, their wings beating the air. Bud tries to chase them, but after a while he comes back, his tongue hanging out of his mouth, and allows Nan to tie him back to the lead.

"Does he chase foxes?" I ask.

"No, he's a bird dog."

Bud catches another scent and forgets he is tired. Nan has about as much weight as a butterfly and is pulled along. I run with her and suddenly feel weightless, as if there were no burden of knowledge to hold me down.

Three

Sometimes it seems things go along and nothing ever happens, and then all of a sudden one thing comes on top of another, or maybe because of it, like a stack of dominoes falling. That's how it seems when Tom elopes the week after Adra leaves. Mama was more upset than Daddy, I guess, since she thinks the world of Tom and doesn't believe anybody will ever be good enough for him. Daddy gets used to the idea of Tom being married before Mama does and makes arrangements with Aunt Opal to rent them part of her house, since she has rooms she doesn't use. Even Mama thinks this is a good idea, since Tom will be close.

Tom's elopement is all anyone talks about all week. It seems like everyone has forgotten about Adra. People call

Mama asking questions about Lula, what she looks like and who her people are. She tells everyone how happy we are for Tom, and the more she says this, the more she comes to accept the idea that Tom is married, so by the time Tom and Lula come home, Mama is ready to welcome Lula with open arms. I think it helps that both Mama and Daddy think Tom has good judgment, so if he thinks eloping with Lula is sensible, then it must be. Mama hasn't said anything, but she has been looking through baby clothes she has saved. I overheard Aunt Opal, who lives near us, tell Mama she thinks Lula might be going to have a baby. Aunt Opal says there have been more weddings on account of babies than most people know about. Aunt Opal will gossip about everyone she knows, including her own family. Mama is careful what she says around Aunt Opal, knowing her words could wind up being repeated all over town. Aunt Opal is old, and she doesn't have much else to do besides talk. Tom's running off with Lula is like some kind of restorative medicine, since it gives her a whole new subject, and Tom and Lula's moving into one side of her house pleases her no end.

After Tom and Lula finally get back, they set up housekeeping at Aunt Opal's. Lula's sister, Nan, comes to visit after school once or twice a week, and when she does, they always invite me to come over. One Wednesday afternoon, Nan and I are outside in the front yard playing with my old yellow tomcat when Preacher Edwards and his wife come by. She is dressed up just like she might be going to church. He helps her out of the car, and she smooths the pleats of her dress and straightens the string of pearls around her neck, which I bet you anything did not come from the Sears Roebuck catalog. She probably has gone clear to the ocean to get those pearls.

I don't want to talk to her, so I pet the cat and try to pretend I haven't noticed her at all.

She walks up to us and says, "Hello, Cassie, I haven't met your friend."

It is only manners to introduce Nan, and manners don't take into account how a person feels. "This is Nan, Lula's sister. My cat's name is General Robert E. Lee."

"I'm delighted to meet the both of you." She smiles and bends down, reaching her hand out toward the General, asking, "May I pet him?"

The General is not known for being accommodating of strangers. He hisses and raises his back fur.

Mrs. Edwards looks hurt as she pulls her hand back, so I say, "Sorry, I guess he's just particular sometimes."

"It's all right. I often wish I had that privilege." She stands up, saying, "It was nice to meet you, Nan."

Lula is at the door waiting and invites her into the parlor, calling to us, "I've just baked some cookies, if you girls would like some."

"Come on, Cassie. I want to go in for a little while," Nan says, trying to pull me up. I resist, but the General doesn't like me tussling with Nan and jumps clear out of my lap. Nan isn't taking no for an answer, so I go along into the house, leaving the General since Lula isn't one for cats in the house.

"What a lovely room," Mrs. Edwards tells Lula. "So open and airy." Lula has just repainted the walls so they are a creamy white color and has hung up lace curtains, which are drawn back from the open window.

Lula goes to get iced tea and a plate of cookies. Aunt Opal knocks on the back door, and Lula invites her in. Aunt Opal likes to come over when Lula has company. Lula has had lots of visitors since moving in, so I guess she can afford to share. Lula comes back into the room with a plate of cookies that are burned around the edges.

Mrs. Edwards selects a cookie, ignoring the burned edges, and says, "What delicious cookies. I never seem to have much luck myself with baking."

Aunt Opal follows Lula into the room and gets settled in the rocking chair. Aunt Opal has a bag she carries with whatever handwork she's working on. Just now it's crocheting, and she draws the needles and yarn from the bag.

Aunt Opal says, "Baking may be a lost art soon. Girls think they don't need to stay home and learn from their mothers."

I nudge Nan to get up to go back outside before Aunt Opal can criticize us directly, but Nan won't budge.

Mrs. Edwards says to Lula, "I wanted to offer congratulations on your marriage. I like Tom tremendously and have been dying to meet you."

"Tom is a fine young man," Aunt Opal cuts in. She hates being left out of the conversation. "Now, his sister Adra is a different story. I wasn't surprised by the way she up and left." Aunt Opal gives a long sigh, but this doesn't mean she's tired. It means she's getting ready to launch into a long-winded story and will not stop until the people listening feel as if they have been through the experience themselves and are like to die from it.

I just wish she wasn't talking about my sister. I guess Lula feels the same, for she tries to steer Aunt Opal in another direction by saying, "I haven't lived here but a few weeks, but I already feel at home."

"Living in one place, a person learns the history of everyone who lives here," Aunt Opal says, then turns to Mrs. Edwards, stating the obvious: "You haven't lived here long." I am sure Aunt Opal remembers to the day when the preacher and his wife came to town. Acquiring a preacher who comes all the way from St. Louis is an event not quickly forgotten. The day they came in on the train I'd gone downtown with Tom, and we saw them get off the train. Mrs. Edwards was wearing a fur cape, like someone in the pictures, and she looked up and down the main street, holding her head up like a peacock who got into a chicken coop by mistake.

Mrs. Edwards thinks Aunt Opal is asking when she moved here and says, "We moved here just before summer. It was the same week that boy was killed by the train."

Aunt Opal picks up the strand of conversation like she picks up a crochet stitch. She says, "That would have been Ben Hammond—Adra's boyfriend. He sang solos down at the church sometimes—had a real pretty voice. His mama never got over it. She wasn't well before it happened, and now her mind is about gone."

Lula interrupts, "Would you like some more tea?"

Aunt Opal ignores her and says, "Some people say it was because of Adra he killed himself, though I don't reckon anyone will ever know for certain."

"That's not true at all. Adra loved Ben," I speak up, even though children are not supposed to take part in grown-up conversations. It's an effort to stop Aunt Opal, but you could as soon stop a freight train as stop Aunt Opal from talking.

Aunt Opal goes on, "Still, when something happens, it's usually the girl that's at fault, ever since Eve talked Adam into eating that apple."

Mrs. Edwards looks as if she's stymied for a moment and then says in a dry voice, "I always feel that Eve has taken more than her fair share of the blame for that particular sin. It seems to me that Adam could have refused."

I am struck all of a sudden by an image of Mrs. Edwards holding an apple out for my Daddy. I close my eyes tight to erase the picture, and Lula must notice, for she touches my arm as if to see if I'm all right.

Aunt Opal doesn't know what to make of this, so she says, "Never mind Adam and Eve. I can tell you Adra didn't cry at his funeral. Not one tear. Not even when they sang 'When the Roll Is Called Up Yonder,' and no one knew whether Ben would be called up yonder, if he walked onto that track deliberate."

"Adra must have been devastated," Mrs. Edwards says.

I don't know what to think. I can't just hate the preacher's wife the way I would like to, when she's taking Adra's side against Aunt Opal. I slip outside and scoop up the General in my arms, and we settle down on the back steps. I can still hear Aunt Opal talking.

"Adra used to go off with a group of them, dancing and carrying on. Wouldn't come home till morning. No one could do a thing with her." Aunt Opal is full of condemnation, but it is lost on Mrs. Edwards.

"I simply didn't realize what a strain she was under. I wish I could have done something to help."

I feel tears start in my eyes, unaccountably, for I have no reason to be upset. I bury my face in the General's warm fur. Aunt Opal does not know one thing about how Adra felt. She only cares about gossiping about people. Adra must have heard the voices gossiping about her, cold and merciless as the wind in winter. I can't blame her for going off. She is not likely to come back to our town, where people have long memories of things that are not exactly true. I would look elsewhere for kindness and warmth if I were Adra, not here.

Nan comes out now, carrying cookies in a napkin, and hands me one. She sits down next to me and is quiet for a little before she asks, "Is your aunt a blood relation?"

"No. She married Mama's older brother, Wilbur. He's been dead a long time. Come on, let's not sit here any longer."

"Your aunt doesn't care much for your sister."

I hadn't thought about this. You always think your relatives will stick by you, but maybe Adra hurt Aunt Opal's feelings. Adra wasn't always patient and didn't put up with much.

We walk away from the house. Though it's late afternoon the day is still warm, and we walk barefoot through ankle-deep grass that Tom hasn't gotten around to cutting.

Nan seems to sense I'm thinking about Adra and is silent, giving me time to remember. I helped Adra pack. She left most of her things behind. She said she wouldn't take anything she couldn't carry herself. Adra's suitcase was brand-new, with brass locks. I went with her when she bought it at a store in Fort Smith.

Adra had arranged her clothes in her suitcase carefully,

as if she'd given the matter some thought beforehand. I'd asked her then, "You'll come back?"

"I don't know when."

"You'll write?"

"Not right away. I can't be looking back—do you understand?"

I didn't want to disappoint her, so I nodded.

"Listen," Adra had said. "If I stayed here, I'd always be the person they expect me to be. I am planning on doing something with my life." She looks ready for a fight, though she is only talking to me, which she must notice, for the anger that came so sudden goes, as quick as it came.

"I don't know why you have to go off. Is it because of what happened to Ben?"

Adra sits down on the bed beside me and says, "Partly, I guess. Sometimes I still can't believe what happened. Sometimes I imagine I see Ben coming down the road toward the house like he used to."

She changes her tone then and says in a lighter voice, "Don't worry, it will be all right. You are frowning just like Mama. Keep that up, and you'll wind up with wrinkles before you're sixteen."

It's not worry, but a wish I could go with her. I don't ask. I don't want to listen to reasons why I cannot. Instead I try to memorize her, so I won't forget once she's gone.

Nan says, "Tell me about your sister, Adra?"

I swish my feet through the long grass and look off down the alley toward the railroad track and think about Adra climbing up the steps of the train carrying her new suitcase. She'd look straight ahead, and anyone would think she knew exactly where she was going.

"Adra always did things first, even before Tom."

"Like Lula," Nan says.

"I guess. She was always brave. She'd stand up to Daddy if Jake or I was in trouble. You knew you could count on her."

Nan wanders over to the rope swing that Tom put up for us. Tom used a thick rope that looks good and strong, so even when I swing high toward the branches, I don't worry it will break. Nan pulls herself up on the swing like a bird lighting on a perch and then pushes off with her foot to twist the swing in a full circle.

"Ben, the boy who died, what was he like?"

"He was real quiet and kept to himself. They never held hands when he came to see her. They'd study together or talk. Even when he walked her home at night, I never saw them kissing." I remember Ben and Adra walking together, how Ben would lean toward Adra while they talked in a serious way, not noticing which way they were going.

And I remember the night before Ben died, when Adra came home crying, so I thought something terrible had happened. I could hear Mama and Adra talking, since the wall between our rooms is paper-thin. I can still remember what Adra said, her voice small with pain, how she said there must be something terribly wrong with her, for Ben couldn't bear to touch her.

The next day we heard the news that Ben was dead. And it wasn't long after that Adra began changing and started running around with the wild kids at school. That much Aunt Opal said was true. I think Adra might have been trying to lose herself. Now she's gone farther away and probably is changing even more. When she comes home, maybe no one will know her but me.

Four

Saturday morning I am out walking, not paying any attention to where I'm going, since I don't have anywhere special to go. Sometimes I walk and walk, and don't notice where I am, and then when I come to, I'm surprised how far I've come. It's not like sleepwalking, on account of I'm awake. It's more like I'm walking in thoughts or dreams and don't really see what's in front of me. Until I'm climbing Brown's Hill, on the road that leads out of town, when I hear the crunch of gravel behind me and turn and there's Jake coming, pumping his bike furiously so the sack of groceries in his basket sways from one side to the other. He is not going to let the hill get the better of him. Jake delivers groceries on Saturdays, and they pay him a whole dollar. I wish they'd let me, but nobody hires girls.

From the top of the hill I can see the whole town, and that's where I wait for Jake.

Jake brakes hard and stops right in front of me, but I stand my ground. The best way to get along with Jake is never to show fear.

"Hey, kid, where do you think you're going?" Jake asks.

"No place special."

"If you want, I'll ride you. Climb on." Jake gestures to-ward the back fender as if his bike were a gallant steed and I were a princess. "I've got one more delivery to make."

I climb on, swinging my legs wide so they don't get in the spokes, and hold on to the seat of the bike. It's down-hill, and we pick up speed fast, so it feels like flying, as if we might lift up and take off. Jake is a madman. I need to remember this so I don't make the same mistake twice. He weaves around a deep hole in the road, gravel flying up from the tires. We reach the bottom of the hill, and Jake slows down to turn on a dirt road that cuts through the woods. At the end of the road is Ben Hammond's house. If I had guessed where Jake was going, I wouldn't have come with him.

Jake stops the bike when we reach the Hammonds' yard, where the weeds come up as high as the bike's tires. Jake says, "I have to take this up to the house. You can wait here if you want to."

"I'll come with you," I offer, even though I'd just as soon wait. I'd hate for Jake to guess I'm afraid of going up there. People say Mrs. Hammond has done lost her mind and talks real crazy. She doesn't go anywhere, just rocks on the porch. Ben was her only son, and she was old when she had him, past forty, so she's pretty old now.

The house is covered over with wisteria vines on one side, and they trail around the porch rails. Sure enough, Mrs. Hammond is out on the porch. As we come closer we can hear the creaking of the rocker. Otherwise it is quiet, except for the cooing of a mourning dove off in the woods back of the house.

Mrs. Hammond sees us coming, but she doesn't call out the way people do, just lifts her hands in the air and then they fall back in her lap. She doesn't smile, just stares at us. She's not as old as Aunt Opal, but she looks older. Aunt Opal is always dressed for company and would never sit on the porch unless she had on her earrings and necklace. Mrs. Hammond is wearing an old housedress, but it's buttoned wrong so the material is bunched up in places, and has tied her hair, which is long and a yellow-white color, back in a rag. Her eyes are light blue, and she fixes them on me so it is hard to move at all.

She finally says, "Devil's child. I have been expecting you. Come closer so I can speak to you."

I don't move, not one step.

Mrs. Hammond gets up out of the rocker and leans against the porch rail. She says, "I've seen the look of that one before. Get behind me, Satan."

She thrusts a long bony finger in my direction, and I feel cold, though the sun is beating right down on us. Jake acts as if nothing unusual is going on and walks up the porch steps and puts the sack down. He says, "Here's your groceries." He turns around and comes back to where I stand as if I'm transfixed.

Her eyes are fixed right on me and don't blink once, so that her face looks like it has frozen in a place where there is no light shining, where even memory doesn't carry kindness.

"You are cursed. Like my son that's dead."

Jake grabs my hand and pulls me out of the yard. I don't look back. I am afraid she could turn me to stone. I wish I could run and get clear away, but I am not going to act afraid. Not while I am walking beside Jake.

Going back Jake pushes his bike up the hill, since it's too steep for him to bike with me on the back. He could probably ride back up if it were just him on the bike. It's coming on toward dusk, and coming up the hill we are in shadow, for the sun has gone over on the other side of the mountain.

"Don't pay any attention to that old woman," Jake says finally.

"Is she always like that?"

"Mostly she never says anything at all, at least not to me. None of the other delivery boys like to come this way."

"Is it because of Ben's dying and all, why she's like that?" I ask Jake.

Jake frowns. "I can't remember her acting so crazy before Ben died."

"I wonder what happened to Ben, if he went crazy, if that's why he did it."

"Who knows? Ben was different, I guess, but I never thought he was crazy. Even though he hung around with the other kids, he was kind of separate. He liked Adra best, but I don't think he liked her the way she liked him."

I think about this. Adra used to wait for Ben to come over, and if he was late she'd be in a state. He was always real quiet when he stopped to see Adra, and you couldn't tell how he was feeling.

Jake muses, "Ben and me, we used to go fishing sometimes. I just wish I'd have got him to go fishing that day and we'd have stayed at the lake way past the time for the trains to run."

We reach the top of the hill, and sure enough the sun is still in the sky, and we are back into the world of daylight. Jake offers me a seat on back of the bike, and I don't think twice about getting back on. We sail down the hill toward town, away from the dark side of the mountain where Mrs. Hammond sits on her porch.

Five

I've never seen a gypsy before, though I have heard tales about gypsies with black hair and black eyes who travel around the country telling fortunes and stealing the shirt off your back. So when I come upon the girl wearing a long red skirt who has a bandanna holding her long black hair in place, I imagine she is a gypsy child. She is shaking the branches of an apple tree as if her life depended upon it and doesn't seem to mind the apples falling like hailstones. She hasn't seen me, so I begin whistling. I hate someone sneaking up on me. She darts a fierce look in my direction as if she thinks I'm going to steal her apples.

I have a cord of licorice in my pocket that Jake gave me. I pull it out and tear it in half, offering her a piece. She takes it and puts it into the pocket of her skirt.

"You want help carrying those apples?" I figure this is my chance to see gypsies and maybe get a fortune-teller to tell my fortune. Maybe a gypsy fortune-teller could read in her crystal ball where Adra's gone and see what she's doing now.

She doesn't answer, but instead looks off where a tall boy, with the same dark hair, is coming through a patch of scrub pines. I know him from school. His name is Jan Varga, and he's in my class though he's fifteen, two years older than me. His family crossed the ocean to come here from Hungary. How they wound up in Arkansas is a wonder. I heard Tom, who gets to know most everyone in town when they come into the store, telling Mama that first they went to New York and from there on to Chicago, where they lived in a tenement house. Jan's daddy had a hard time making a living in Chicago. When they heard there were good jobs working on the railroad in Arkansas, Jan's family moved down here, looking for work. Only when they got here, there wasn't any work at all. Then Jan's mother got sick, so they stopped here, and Jan's father got a job in town that nobody else wanted. He's what's called a scavenger, which means he cleans people's outhouses at night and hauls away refuse. Tom says it's a fair-paying job that everyone who was born here thinks they are too good to do.

You can hear Jan and his father coming by at night. Jan comes to school smelling like lye soap and is probably the cleanest boy in school. Lots of kids come to school dirty. I would swear the Carver kids have never sat in a number-two tub in their whole life. I had to sit next to Mikey Carver one entire year, so I am sure this is so. At school, no one pays much attention to Jan. He sits at the back of the room and reads books and is so quiet you forget he's there at all.

Just now, though, he is frowning. "Katia, I have been looking all over for you. You know you shouldn't come up here. There is a sign posted."

"It is wasteful to leave the apples," she says as she lifts the sack of apples over her shoulder, then walks away without looking back.

I am sorry to see her go, and even sorrier she is not a gypsy like I thought.

Jan says, "My sister—you cannot tell her anything."

I break off a piece of licorice from the half I have left and offer it to Jan, saying, "My brother Jake is the same. He won't listen to anyone who tells him what to do."

Jan takes a bite of licorice and says, "I have noticed this."

For a minute I wonder if I should be talking about Jake like this, while eating licorice he gave me, then figure he wouldn't really care. After all, I haven't said anything that isn't true.

There is a noise of someone coming, pushing through the thicket below us. It's Robert Morgan, who owns this land.

I have never seen him up this high on the mountain. He's carrying a shotgun.

"You kids been stealing my apples? I don't aim to tell you again." He lifts the gun and points it straight at us. Jan grabs my wrist and pulls me away into the bushes.

Robert Morgan doesn't bother to chase us, just fires off his shotgun as we run weaving downhill until I am out of breath and fall to the ground.

"He had no right to shoot at us like that," I say as soon as I catch my breath.

Jan says, "You would tell him so while he points a gun at you?"

"I would have if you hadn't pulled me away. He'd have known who I was and not dared shoot us. He'd know my daddy would come after him if anything happened to me."

"Next time I will leave you there and let Robert Morgan shoot you," Jan says, but there is a teasing note to his voice that lets me know he doesn't mean it.

"There's laws against shooting people. I'm going to tell my daddy so the sheriff can arrest him."

"No sheriff," Jan says, looking worried. "It would only be trouble."

"All right." I guess he thinks his sister might be in trouble for stealing apples and thinks Robert Morgan has the right to shoot at them. If this is how he thinks people here act, no wonder he barely talks at school.

The next day at school during recess I find Jan outside reading in the shade of an oak tree. Kids don't talk to him much. Someone who came from another town wouldn't have an easy time of it, much less someone from across the ocean. You'd think people would be interested in someone who comes from far away and has different experiences, but I guess they are afraid some of the difference will wear off on them.

He closes his book and gestures with his hand an invitation to sit down on the grass next to him.

Girls of thirteen don't go sit beside a boy, but Jan is so different, it seems to me the unspoken rules just don't apply. I doubt if Jan even knows there are rules how girls are supposed to act.

"You know, most folks around here wouldn't shoot at us the way Robert Morgan did yesterday. He's mean and crazy. He owns lots of land he inherited from his daddy, and whenever he needs money, he sells some trees to the lumber company." I don't tell Jan how it worries me that one day I might go climbing up the hills and find the trees gone.

"That is too bad," Jan says. "Where I came from there are forests of beech and oak trees, and when you walk deep into the forest you feel as if you were walking into an older time. I would be sorry to see those trees cut down."

I wonder how Jan and his family came to leave their

home. Jan sounds as if he misses where he came from. I guess if I left here, I'd be homesick for more than my family. I'd miss walking over the hills and scrambling over the creeks. I'd miss the line of mountains you can see from my front porch, and I can't imagine leaving all the people I know.

Jan lies back against the trunk of the tree, closing his eyes, talking quietly so only I can hear. "The trees have wide trunks and many branches with bright green leaves. They seem as if they would shelter you from harm. And there is a river running through the forest, and it is the color of the sky. It is so wide you cannot swim across."

I am imagining I am walking along this river, sheltered by the trees and feeling quite peaceful listening to Jan talk, when my brother Jake strides up and takes hold of my wrist, pulling me up.

"Leave me alone!"

"Don't you be talking to him." Jake gestures at Jan.

"I'll talk to whomever I please."

"No, you won't. He's foreign and a thief," Jake says, and pulls me up.

Cary, Cal, and Wayne have come up and stand watching Jake so he can't back down.

Jake says, "Robert Morgan said they've been stealing his apples."

"Robert Morgan is crazy. He shot at us yesterday when I was up on the mountain."

"Darn it, Cassie, you shouldn't go off wandering by yourself up on the mountain."

Jan stands up and says, "Cassie was only out walking. Let her alone."

Even the girls in my class have come over now and stand a little apart, whispering. Marylou whispers so everyone can hear, "Her sister had to go away."

Some of the other girls lean in, listening, though I don't see Lizzie among them. Marylou pretends to whisper, but means for her voice to carry. "You can't keep a baby a secret. It starts to show after a few months. Everybody knows that's why her sister left town."

I wrench my arm free from Jake's grip, furious with Marylou as much as with Jake.

If Jake has heard Marylou, he doesn't show it.

Marylou isn't whispering now. She says, "Runs in the family, I guess. After all, she was up on the mountain with him."

Jake can't ignore what Marylou is saying any longer, but instead of telling Marylou off, he goes after Jan.

"Stay away from my sister," Jake says.

"Cassie is my friend." Jan speaks in a calm voice, seemingly unaware that Jake is fighting mad and all his friends are standing around hopeful of a fight. Then I see Jan's fists are clenched, though his arms are hanging loose at his sides, and I wonder if he is going to fight Jake.

Jake lunges at Jan, thrusting a fist at his chest. At the

same time I cut between Jan and Jake, pushing Jake's arm so he misses Jan. Then, because I'm in the way and Jake doesn't want to hit me, Jake falls down, taking me to the ground instead of Jan.

Across the schoolyard I can see Lizzie, who's gone to get Mr. Turner. "Stop that right now!" Mr. Turner yells as he comes running up. Mr. Turner coaches boy's basketball and is used to pulling players apart. He pulls Jake up and takes my elbow.

"You both are staying after school!"

Jake glares at me, and normally I'd be upset, only what Marylou has been saying about Adra has me so mad I can't bother with Jake. Marylou tells lies in whispers, and the other girls all listen. I look over and see Lizzie standing next to Marylou. She wouldn't have heard what Marylou said about Adra. I don't know why she went after Mr. Turner, but I'm glad she did. I sure didn't want Jan to have to fight on account of me.

Mr. Turner marches us back into the schoolroom, and I glance back. Jan is watching me, and he looks worried. Then he smiles and gives me a thumbs-up sign, and I don't feel so bad.

Jake and I are kept after school by Miss Hallifax, the first-grade teacher. We are the only students kept after school and have the room to ourselves. Miss Hallifax is at her desk working on some papers, and I don't believe she is happy to have our company, judging by the looks she gives us, which make it clear we are no longer first-graders and don't belong in her room. Jake fidgets, trying to get comfortable in a desk that is too small for him, and his legs knock over a wastebasket out in the aisle between the desks. Miss Hallifax raises her ruler in a manner that leaves no doubt as to her intentions. Jake tries to fold his legs under the chair, looking so uncomfortable that I'd feel sorry for him, except it's his fault we are stuck staying after school. Since I'm smaller than Jake, sitting in a desk built for a six-year-old is not an act of physical torture, but I still have a hard time sitting still.

I keep thinking about what Marylou said about Adra and how she left town because she was going to have a baby. Well, that is just plain crazy. Adra left because she wanted to forget about Ben and how he died. I know that. And I know Marylou loves telling tales, partly for attention and partly for spite. She is never going to forgive me for kicking her, and maybe I don't blame her, if I think about it.

The only thing Marylou said that has a grain of truth in it is that it takes a long time before having a baby shows on a person. There is no sign at all that Lula is going to have a baby, but now we all know it because Tom and Lula have said so. Lula is already letting out the seams in some of her dresses, though it's going to be some months before she needs them. I didn't see Adra let out the seams on any of her dresses.

Time passes slowly during this long hour in a silent room, with only the sound of Miss Hallifax shuffling papers at her desk. Jake doesn't glance in my direction, which is unusual. He is not one to stay mad.

When Miss Hallifax tells us our time is up, Jake dashes outside. I gather my things and nod a good-bye at Mrs. Hallifax, who is not particularly interested, since it has been so long since we were in the first grade, she's forgotten us.

Jake's friends are all waiting for him across the street from the school.

"Jake's a sissy. He lets his sister get in his way instead of fighting," Cal calls out.

Jake steps in front of Cal, raising his fists. The four boys form a circle around Jake and Cal, hopeful of a fight.

Then Jake looks across at the school where I stand on the steps, uncurls his fists, and says, "I was going to fight Jan. Cassie just got in the way." Jake looks directly at Cary. "You wouldn't hit your sister, would you, if she was in the way?"

Jake waits, sticking his thumbs into his suspenders, letting them consider. Cary shifts from one foot to another. Cary looks so much like Jake they could be brothers, only there is no relationship between our families as far as I know. Cary for sure wouldn't hit his sister, because she is built like a tank and bigger than he is.

Cal says, "No girl lives who can knock me down."

Jake sucks in his breath and folds his arms across his chest. He says, "Cassie did not knock me down. She only got me off balance, and we both fell."

It looks as if Jake doesn't really want to fight Cal, but I figure he's going to have to. His gang has the politics of a wolf pack. If the leader shows any sign of weakness, someone will challenge him. I expect Cal sees this as his chance to take over.

Cal's voice has grown raucous, like the crows in the tops of the trees hoping for death and a meal. "Jake's a girl. Jake's a girl. Sissy sissy girl," he chants.

"He is not," Wayne says. Wayne is loyal, and though not particularly quick, he is strong and can push over an outhouse by himself, though I have never heard tell of him being in a fight with anyone.

"Cal, I'll whip you if you call me a girl one more time," Jake says.

Cal steps up to Jake, his fists raised, and says, "I'm not afraid of you. You can't even look out for your own sister. If I had a sister, I wouldn't let her go off in the woods with some foreigner."

Jake just stands there as if struck by the words like they were blows. Cary is looking away, as if he is embarrassed. I guess they are all thinking of what Marylou said. Jake looks around, then he sees me watching. He gives me a look that says, Get lost now, and turns back to the others.

He says, "You'all meet me tonight at the churchyard at midnight, and we'll see who's a sissy." Jake's voice is cold, and he doesn't sound angry, but as if he's come to some decision that I would bet has nothing to do with Cal. No one answers Jake. I expect they will show up at the churchyard at midnight. After all, they wouldn't want anyone to think they were scared.

When I go up to bed, I don't undress, just get in bed with the quilt pulled up to my chin. I am not one bit sleepy for worrying about what Jake is going to do tonight when he meets his friends in the churchyard. I have decided to follow him. I know he slips out of his room using a rope ladder, but I figure I can go right out the front door. Mama and Daddy go to bed about ten o'clock and sleep so hard they'd sleep through a tornado.

About eleven-thirty I hear Jake moving around, so I get out of bed and wait until I hear the soft thud of the rope ladder against the house before I slip downstairs, carrying my shoes. I wait, watching from the front window, until I see Jake. He's walking down the middle of the road, not worried about anyone seeing him in the moonlight. He walks confidently, as if he is sure the night belongs to him.

I follow Jake, keeping a good distance between us. At the edge of the churchyard I leave the road and cut through the graveyard. Wayne and Cary are huddled in the shadows next to the church, while Cal stands out in the open, smoking a cigarette, the spark of light glowing. I hide behind the headstones, moving closer, using the gravestones and trees as shelter.

"Cal said you wouldn't come out, that you were scared to fight him," Wayne says. "I knew you'd come."

Jake says, "I don't have call to fight you, Cal. I intend to fight Jan so he'll know to keep away from my sister."

Though Jake is my brother, and I know he thinks he's looking out for me, it is hard to believe how dumb he can be. Somehow he had determined that fighting Jan is a good idea and will not only protect me but impress his friends.

Jake says, "Jan will be out working with his daddy, but some of the time he works alone. Now, I don't want you fellows scaring him off, so you keep a ways back."

I wish I'd never run into Jan and his sister up on the mountain or gone over to talk to Jan at school. I have managed to cause him trouble when all he wanted was to be left alone.

Jake leads off, and they all follow, strung out behind Jake looking like a pack of wolves. I wonder if there is any way I can find Jan first, before Jake does. Jake sneaks out pretty often, though, and probably has a good idea where to find him.

Jake doesn't hesitate at the crossroads but turns left toward the road where Aunt Opal lives. I expect that Jake knows the nighttime world as well as the day, knows whose dogs will bark if they get close and who is likely to come out late at night and smoke on the porch. Out in the woods, up the hill above town, you can hear the cry of a hoot owl. Jake stops as if listening. I'm afraid Jake will turn around and see me, so I dart into Lizzie Miller's backyard.

What Jake hears is the ring of horse hooves on the paved road that runs from the Millers' house on down Main Street. The sound is getting fainter, and I hope Jan's father has finished his rounds and is on his way home. Jake takes off toward the sound. I cut through Lizzie's yard into the alley, and then I see Jan a little ways away, spreading lime around an outhouse. If I'm quick, I can reach Jan before Jake does.

Jan looks up, surprised to see me come running through the Millers' yard. Jan stops working and says, "Cassie, what is wrong?"

"My brother Jake is out looking for you right now. He wants to fight."

"Why? I have done nothing to him."

"He's showing off for his friends. They gave him a hard time saying things about our being in the woods."

"Because I am a foreigner?"

"I guess." I look off down the alley. I wish people wouldn't let things like where a person is from matter so much.

"You came out alone to tell me," Jan says, as if he is still surprised. "My sister is afraid of the dark."

Jan lifts his head as if listening. They are coming back.

"It will be trouble if they find you with me." Jan opens the door to the outhouse and takes my elbow. "Wait in here."

It's dark inside the outhouse after being out in the moonlight. The door is open just a crack, but it is enough so I can see Jan stand, holding the shovel high across his chest like a weapon. Jake is walking up the alley while Cary, Wayne, and Cal follow behind. The way Jan stands, resigned and waiting, I guess he figures he will have to fight them all.

Jake stops a few feet away, uncertain because of the way Jan holds the shovel, as if he means to use it. Jan wouldn't know that it is Jake only who wants to fight him, and that Jake always fights bare-fisted.

Jake says, "Cary, you and Cal and Wayne, get back. This is between me and Jan."

Jan says, "I have no reason to fight with you."

Jake answers, "I have reason enough. Will you fight?"

Jan lets the shovel slide down so it rests on the ground, but so he sort of leans on it. "No, I don't want to fight you." His fingers are wound tight around the shovel, but that is the only sign of tension. He's leaning on the shovel as if he's relaxed.

I can't believe it is this simple that someone could just

refuse to fight. Boys don't do this. They are always fighting about something at school, at ball games, and even after church.

Jake, disgusted, kicks at the ground with his foot. I don't think he ever imagined Jan wouldn't fight him. Jan turns his back on Jake and goes back to work with the shovel, spreading lime around the outhouse.

Cal stoops and picks up a rock and throws it hard, hitting Jan between the shoulder blades. It makes a dull thud against Jan's quilted jacket and falls to the ground. Jan goes on shoveling as if it were only a pebble and of no consequence.

Jake is dumbfounded for an instant, not sure who he wants to fight. I can see he's furious, for his face is turning red. He turns and tackles Cal, who has another rock in his hand, yelling, "Are you crazy, throwing rocks? And this is my fight, not yours."

Jake has Cal on the ground, and they are both kicking and punching and yelling. It's enough to wake the dead, and it sure wakes up the living. Lights are coming on in the houses up and down the alley, and Lizzie Miller's father yells out the window, "I"m calling the sheriff."

Wayne, who never fights, hears this and grabs hold of Jake, pulling him away from Cal. "Stop fighting. The sheriff is coming." Wayne and Cary drag Jake down the alley, while Cal takes off in the other direction. Lizzie Miller's father slams down the window, and lights go off in the houses. The only sound is the breeze high in the trees and the soft sound of the shovel.

Jan opens the door and helps me out, saying, "It is safe now."

"Are you all right?" I touch the quilted padding of Jan's jacket where the rock hit him.

"It was only a small rock. I will walk you home."

"You don't have to."

"You are brave to come out alone in the dark, to follow your brother, who would be angry with you. I want to walk you home. I don't think we will run into Jake now."

"All right." I had been so worried about what Jake might do that it seems funny not to be thinking of Jake at all. Instead I am thinking about Jan and how he stood up, unafraid of Jake and his friends. As the wind turns cooler, I shiver. Jan notices and puts an arm across my shoulder. I feel a kind of warmness growing inside me, and it seems as if the road through the town has become a journey in a fairy tale, as we walk through the silent nighttime world past the dark houses, walking on the same road I always walk, only everything looks different in the bright moonlight, as if I can see everything more clearly, as if in the daytime world I am asleep and only now have I come alive.

Six

❧

I wake up early Saturday morning to the sound of voices in the kitchen. It's Tom, who stops by some mornings to visit with Mama and eat breakfast. Lula hasn't quite gotten the knack of cooking, at least not to fix biscuits the way Mama does. Mama likes fixing breakfast for Tom, for then it seems as if he has not grown up and moved away from home, although he has not gone far—less than a mile. I wonder if Tom is talking about the ruckus last night, so I pull on my clothes and go on down to the kitchen.

"Morning, Cassie," Tom says. "You are up early—early bird gets the worm."

"I'm not looking for worms. I just came down before you eat all of Mama's biscuits."

"There's more than enough biscuits," Mama says.

Tom smears blackberry jam on a biscuit and says, "You wouldn't believe all the commotion going on last night. I woke up and heard Bill Miller, who lives down the way, yelling like blazes. All I could think was someone's house had caught fire, so I pulled on my britches and ran outside but couldn't see there was anything amiss."

"It's good you're living over at Opal's. I used to worry about her living all by herself," Mama says.

Tom finishes his breakfast and carries his plate to the sink, then sits back down and listens to Mama worry about Aunt Opal, while I relax. Tom didn't see us, and Mama has no idea Jake sneaks out at night. Once Jake drank some moonshine whiskey and was sick the next day. I knew, but I would never tell. Mama thinks one day Jake will grow up and be sensible like Tom, only Tom has always been sensible, even when he was Jake's age. Tom is only seven years older than me, and I can remember. It doesn't seem to me a person becomes sensible just because he gets older. Mama is doomed to disappointment if she's waiting for Jake to grow up and turn sensible.

Tom says, "The preacher's wife came calling the other day. Lula liked her real well, said she wasn't snooty like she'd heard."

Mama gets up and goes to the sink to wash dishes. She says, "I expect it's hard to come from a city to a little town. She's used to being around people she doesn't know to speak to, and now she's expected to speak to everyone she meets. If she forgets now and then, people think it's on purpose and hold it against her."

I wonder if Mama is thinking about Adra having left a town where she knows everyone to live in a city where she doesn't know a soul and no one knows who she is.

Tom says, "Lula has invited the preacher and his wife to Sunday dinner. She can't decide what to cook."

Mama says, "I'll stop by later. I'm going to bake today and bring an apple pie over to Lula. You can have that for dessert."

"Thanks, Mama. I'd better be off," Tom says, going on to work.

I finish breakfast and help Mama with the dishes, then go outside on the porch. I expect I should help Mama if she is going to bake. Adra would have if she were here, though I expect I would just get in the way. If I leave quietly, Mama will not notice me going, and I can walk down to the post office. One day a letter from Adra will come.

I am glad Mama feels like baking again. Right after Adra left, it seemed like she stayed in the bedroom with the door closed, not sleeping, but just lying in bed with her eyes open. Now that Tom is married, and Lula is so pitiful a cook, she is always cooking something and carrying it over to Tom and Lula's house. Tom doesn't care that Lula is a terrible cook. I've heard Aunt Opal say that cooking is the way to a man's heart, but it sure looks like there are other ways. I am pretty sure that Mrs. Edwards has never cooked anything for my daddy.

Mama hasn't called me back in, so I skedaddle down the porch steps and on down the road, not stopping until I am clear of the house and out of calling distance. It's a warm day, and above me the sky is just swirling with white cottony clouds. There's cotton growing in a field outside town, only the cotton on those plants is not nearly as white and fluffy as the clouds swirling above my head.

As I pass Lizzie Miller's house, I stop and look down the alley where we were last night and think about how Jan walked me home. I have been keeping thoughts about Jan clear to the back of my mind, a kind of secret from myself, but knowing all the time they are there waiting until I am ready to think. So I am standing in the street, looking for all the world like a person who is lost, when Lizzie comes out on the porch, wearing a bright red dress with a lace collar.

"Hey, Lizzie," I call out, as if she'd never told me she was too grown up to be playing childish games last summer.

"Hi, Cassie. Do you want to come in and see what I got for my birthday?"

"All right."

"I've something to show you."

Show off more likely, I think, but still I follow her inside. Lizzie's house is bigger than most in town, so big her mother needs help to clean it and has Mrs. Connelly come in twice a week. Lizzie doesn't help and isn't expected to. Lizie's role in life is just being Lizzie.

There is a wide entrance and hallway with a staircase that curves into the upstairs part of the house. All along the walls are framed landscapes of mountains and streams like you find up in the Ozarks, which Lizzie's mother has painted herself. I am always amazed at how real they look.

"Hurry up, Cassie," Lizzie calls out, and I wonder what I am doing in Lizzie's house. The hallway smells of furniture polish, and you couldn't find a speck of dust if your life depended on it.

"Happy birthday," I tell Lizzie. I guess I should have remembered Lizzie's birthday, since she's had parties before.

"I'm not having a party this year," Lizzie admits, as if she's just read my mind, and her voice is almost apologetic. "This is my present." Lizzie walks over to a Victrola in a white-enameled case and puts on a record. "Here, I'll show you how it sounds."

Lizzie turns the crank, and music blares out across the room. Lizzie twirls around the room in time to the music. Baptists aren't allowed to dance new dances like the Charleston, although they can square-dance, which for some reason is not considered real dancing. Lizzie's bed has a pure white bedspread, which I figure it's better not to sit on, so I settle down on the cushions on the window seat. When the music stops, Lizzie takes a breath and comes over and sits down beside me.

"Now you have to tell me everything that has happened," Lizzie says, as if we are still best friends who've just spent time away from one another.

"Everything that happened," I repeat, wondering what in particular she wants to know about. So much has happened, I wouldn't know where to begin if I trusted Lizzie, which I don't.

"You know, about you and Jan. I heard you had a rendezvous on top of the mountain, and Robert Morgan discovered the two of you. You might have been killed."

Lizzie's eyes open wide, and it occurs to me she wouldn't have minded if we had been. Lizzie's daddy runs the funeral home, and she considers death as the occasion for a grand funeral. Lizzie goes over to her desk and picks up a book. She says, "It's almost like that play *Romeo and Juliet*. Your daddy would kill you if you took up with a foreigner. That's what the fight with your brother was about, wasn't it?"

"Sort of," I answer, pleased at the idea of my life taking after a play.

Lizzie studies me, so that I almost feel embarrassed wearing Jake's overalls and a faded shirt that used to belong to Adra.

"Who would imagine you would be the first one in our class to have a boyfriend, and a secret one at that? You know, Jan never talks, and I simply had never noticed that he is handsome, isn't he?"

I interrupt Lizzie. "I don't—"

"I saw you last night walking with Jan. Something woke me up, and I couldn't go back to sleep, so I was looking out the window, and that's when I saw you."

Lizzie won't allow me to get a word in, but keeps right on talking. "What a dark horse you turned out to be. I'm so glad you have a boyfriend. We'll have lots to talk about now. His family is Catholic. Catholics worship idols, which is very wrong. Jan's family has a statue of Mary right by their front door. Will you become a Catholic, do you think?"

Lizzie doesn't stop to let me answer her questions, which is a good thing, since I don't know what to say. She lifts a strand of my hair and says, "I know this new way of fixing hair. Will you let me work on yours sometime?" Then she opens her dresser drawer and rummages around looking for something. "I have this new lipstick. Would you like to try it?"

"No!" I say, in a voice that stops Lizzie dead. I realize I've overreacted, when she was just being nice. Lipstick reminds me of the preacher's wife and my daddy.

"Thanks, Lizzie, Mama would about kill me if I came home with lipstick on."

"But you should, Cassie. You'd look swell."

"I'd better go. It's close to ten o'clock, and Mr. Owens

will have the mail in the post office boxes by now. There might be a letter from Adra."

"You haven't heard from her yet?" Lizzie asks, her voice sympathetic.

"We will. She's probably just not settled yet and will write as soon as she is. Oh, thanks for going to get Mr. Turner the other day."

"Normally I wouldn't dream of telling a teacher on someone, but I didn't want Jake to kill your new boyfriend." Lizzie walks downstairs with me to the front door. She says, "Thank you for stopping by. I'll keep your secret."

I know I should tell Lizzie she is dead wrong with all that talk about *Romeo and Juliet*, but I don't. Instead I walk on down Main Street into town, on an ordinary day in the bright sunshine, feeling the road hard and rocky under my feet. Still, it is as if I've entered some new world that is different and where anything may happen.

There are three blocks of stores and offices that make up the downtown. Mostly they are buildings of red brick with large windows, so you can see inside from the sidewalk. On Saturdays lots of people come into town from the country, and there are always groups of people talking on the sidewalk. As I pass the filling station, I wave at the old men who sit outside on the bench, chewing tobacco and telling stories. They are a kind of fixture, always sitting there. I always see people I know downtown, but I'm surprised to see Jan standing outside the drugstore. He has his hair slicked back, and he's wearing a white cotton shirt that looks like it's just been ironed.

"Hi, Cassie," he says, walking up to meet me. "Would you like to have a Coca-Cola at the drugstore?"

"I didn't bring any money," I answer, searching my pockets. I feel scruffy next to him, in my old overalls. I wonder if I combed my hair this morning.

"It's my treat," he says.

"Okay. If you'll let me buy you one sometime."

"If you'd like," Jan says, opening the door to the drug-store.

The drugstore is one of my favorite places to go. I like sitting on the high stools that turn clear around if you want to. There is a mirror so you can see yourself and the people sitting in the booths. And I love the tall glasses and sipping Coca-Cola through a straw. Walking in with Jan, I feel older somehow. I peer into the mirror across the counter to see if I look more grown up than I did at home. I look exactly the same, so you can't go by feelings, I guess.

Mrs. Edwards comes into the drugstore, her arms full of packages. She sees me sitting at the counter and stops to say hello.

"Good morning, Cassie. We seem to frequent the same establishments."

I expect she means seeing me at Lula's earlier this week, and now here. I twist the stool and say, "Hi, do you know

Jan? He's in my class at school." I turn back to Jan, saying, "Meet Mrs. Edwards, our preacher's wife."

Jan slides off the stool and stands. "Hello, I am glad to meet you."

Mrs. Edwards adjusts the bags in her arms and says, "It's delightful to meet such a charming young man. You don't sound as if you come from around here."

"My family moved here last spring."

Mrs. Edwards smiles. "So did I, so we have that in common, being newcomers. I hope to see you again."

Jan seems pleased at the attention, and I don't blame him at all. I would be taken completely by her charm, too, if I had never seen her with my daddy that Sunday morning. It's been only three weeks since we dyed the water, but it seems longer.

She goes to the back of the store to talk to the druggist, and Jan turns back on the stool to face the counter. I watch her laugh at something the druggist has said, and I remember how she clung to my daddy's arm. All of a sudden it strikes me that I blame Mrs. Edwards and not my daddy for what happened. Jan sips his Coca-Cola and does not slurp the way Jake would. He notices how quiet I am and doesn't ask me what I'm thinking. I appreciate this. People are always asking what I'm thinking, and I guess you have layers of thoughts, like clothes. Some go on the outside and some are underneath, too close to the skin.

When my glass is empty, Jan says, "Katia has been helping at home since my mother was sick, but she's going to come to school soon. I wondered if you'd come over to our house so she can get to know you. Then she will know someone when she comes to school and not feel so much a stranger."

"Sure, when?"

"Today?"

We walk slowly down the sidewalk. Two old ladies I recognize from church, Betty and Irene Lowell, walk toward us. Betty pulls Irene back, and both clutch their handbags tight, as if we might be thieves. They stare as we walk by, but I don't think much of this, since they both are odd acting and have always been so. Jan notices and frowns but doesn't say anything. As we walk by the general store where Tom works, I look in the window, but I don't see Tom.

Jan lives at the edge of town in an old house with a ramshackle porch. There's a well for drawing water right on the porch next to the kitchen door.

Katia is hanging clothes on a line while the baby plays on a quilt on the grass. She sees us coming and picks up the baby, leaving the clothes in the basket. She carries the baby, balancing him on her hip easily, and has an air of being sure of herself.

We go inside, and the first thing I notice is how clean everything is. The walls have new white paint, and the wood floors shine. A bright red cloth embroidered with flowers is draped over the sofa.

Katia says their mother is resting upstairs and then asks lots of questions about school. Then she tells Jan, "Go get your violin and play something for Cassie."

As Jan leaves the room, Katia says, "We can talk while he practices."

Jan comes back with his violin in a case and opens it carefully. He cradles the violin under his chin and begins to play, his bow strokes fluid as running water. He doesn't play in the same manner as the fiddlers I've seen at picnics and parties, but uses all of the bow to draw out long sweet notes that sound joyous one moment and full of sorrow the next. Then all of a sudden he begins fiddling, only it is different than the fiddle music I've heard—wilder and faster. Jan's fingers fairly fly over the strings.

Jan seems far away from us, though he's standing a few feet away. I wonder if the music has carried him clear across the ocean to where he came from, if maybe he imagines he is walking in the forest he told me about earlier, where the trees are old as time and where a blue river flows deep into the forest. I let the music carry me, feeling light as if I'm made of air.

Later Jan walks back downtown with me. After putting his violin away, he seemed content to let Katia talk with me and didn't say much. I guess he mainly wanted me to come over for Katia's sake. This is a good trait for a brother to have, to care about his sister. You can't fault that, so I don't know why I should feel disappointed. When we reach the post office, I remember I haven't checked to see if a letter came from Adra. We go in, and I can see our box is empty. Mr. Owens is behind the desk. Mr. Owens probably knows as much about people in town as Aunt Opal. Maybe because people trust him with their mail, they tell him things, or maybe it is because he never talks, just listens patiently.

He shakes his head and says, "Not yet."

I explain to Jan, "My sister Adra left home a few weeks ago. She might write."

Jan asks, "Where is she?"

I look down. I can't answer what should be a simple question. It's strange when someone you care about seems like they've vanished off the face of the earth. There should be a letter with a return address.

Jan seems to sense he's asked the wrong question and says, "Writing letters isn't always the easiest thing when you are beginning a life in a new place."

Jan takes my hand as carefully as he held his violin as we turn off from the main street onto the street by the school.

I can feel the worry about Adra easing away. I look at Jan, but he is looking ahead, and again I feel I am light as air and could twirl in circles the way Lizzie did this morning.

Jan stops beside a hedge that is taller than the both of us and turns to face me directly. He says, "I like you very much, Cassie Hill."

I can feel this shyness come over me, and to hide my feelings I say, "Lizzie said she saw us last night walking in the alley. Lizzie reads a lot and has romantic notions. She imagined us like Romeo and Juliet."

Jan says, "We are like ourselves." Jan leans closer and kisses me on the lips, quick and soft as butterfly wings.

Jan keeps my hand in his until we reach the corner of the road and we can see my house. He stops and says in an almost formal manner, "I am glad you came to talk to Katia. I will see you soon."

"Thank you for playing your violin for me," I say politely, as if he had not kissed me a few minutes ago. I walk up toward my house, and wonder how it was not all that long ago I'd sworn I'd never kiss a boy.

As I come up to the house I see Jake leaning against the side of the house under his bedroom window.

"Cassie, c'mere." Jake's voice is little more than a whisper.

Now that I'm closer, I can see Jake has a black eye, and his shirt is torn and some of the buttons are off. The worn-out expression on his face reminds me of how my tomcat General Robert E. Lee looked the morning he came home after a battle where he lost part of one ear. Jake's ears look to be in place, however.

"Cassie, I need you to go inside and let down the rope ladder that's in my trunk. If Daddy sees me, I'll get a whipping."

"All right." I don't think Jake stands in need of another whipping. Sure enough, Daddy is home and reading in the parlor, where he has a clear view of anyone coming in the front door. I hear Mama in the kitchen, so the back door is out. I wonder how long Jake has waited for me to come home.

Daddy looks up from his book and says, "Where's your brother?"

"I don't know."

"Your mother's been wondering where you both were."

"Well, I've been at Lizzie's and the drugstore—" I stop right there because the first two are acceptable, and who knows what the reaction to visiting Jan might be.

"Go wash, then help your mother in the kitchen."

I take the stairs at a run, duck into Jake's room, and burrow through his trunk, looking for the rope ladder. I tie it to the window, and Jake climbs up. He climbs over the windowsill, and I can tell from the way he moves that he's hurting.

"Tell Mama I don't feel too good, and I'm in bed asleep." Jake takes off his torn shirt and puts on his pajama shirt.

When my cat came home after the battle, he didn't want to be petted. He just wanted to go off and lie down in private and lick his wounds. I guess Jake feels the same.

When I tell Mama Jake is feeling sick, she says, "I didn't hear him come in. To think that poor boy's been lying up there all day sick and no one knew it. I'll go check on him."

"He's fine. He's sleeping."

"It will only take a minute. Go ahead and set the table."

Mama comes back down in a minute, and I can't tell if she saw Jake's black eye or not. She says, "Let me fix a plate of food while you pour him some milk. You can carry his supper up to him."

She fixes him a plate with two pieces of chicken, biscuits and gravy, peas, and mashed potatoes. Then she adds a piece of chocolate cake over to the side and finds a chunk of ice she puts in a cloth.

I carry the plate up to Jake's room, and he begins to eat like a person who hasn't seen food in a long time.

"Mama knows about your eye. She sent you some ice."

"She didn't tell Daddy?"

"Not yet. I think she hates it when he whips us." I hate it when Jake gets a whipping. It doesn't happen very often, but when he does, I can almost feel the sharp sting of the switch on my bare legs, even though I haven't had a whipping in a long time.

"I wonder if Cal looks as bad as you do."

"How'd you know I fought Cal?" Jake asks.

"Lucky guess." I'm not about to let Jake know I followed him the other night.

"Cal beat me, I guess, fair and square, but afterward he went off by himself. Wayne and Cary stuck with me."

"Well, Wayne and Cary are your friends."

"I thought if I fought Cal, he'd stop saying stuff about you and Jan."

"Nobody with any sense pays attention to that Cal," I say, hoping Jake doesn't feel too bad about fighting for something so pointless. I go over and stand by the window. You can see the whole town from here. There's lights in all the houses, and I expect most people are either eating or getting ready to eat supper. Maybe I should feel to blame for Jake's black eye, but I don't. The idea that Jake would fight Cal to stop him from doing or saying something is about like Daddy whipping Jake to get him to behave. A whipping makes Jake a little more secretive and careful not to get caught, and has never yet to my knowledge ever changed him one bit.

Seven

The next day is Sunday, and Jake's eye looks a little better, more of a light purple than black. If anyone asks, he's got a story about how he bumped his head when he got up at night and couldn't see the door was closed. Jake can lie with conviction. I lack conviction even when telling the absolute truth. You can't always believe someone who speaks with conviction. Chances are they may be someone like Jake, just born to tell lies.

Lizzie has that ability. I know this the moment I walk into my Sunday school class and five girls turn their head and stare at me as if I've grown horns and a tail. I figure I've just reached deep water and wonder if I remember how to swim. All I can say for Lizzie is, she might mean to keep a secret when she tells you she will; only she likes to tell things even more than she likes to keep a secret. It's pretty clear they all know I was out in the alley late at night with Jan, and they've heard the dramatic version—Lizzie's version.

Lizzie says, "Cassie, your secret's safe with us."

I take a seat in the row behind Lizzie while the others watch me to see what I have to say.

Betsy turns in her seat and leans over to say, "My mama won't let me go with boys yet. She says I'm too young. I wouldn't dare to sneak out."

Nora says, "My daddy is never going to let me go with boys. He won't even let me wear overalls. He says it's a sin for a woman to dress like a man."

Lizzie says, "Cassie, you are the first to go out with a boy. You have to tell us all about it."

"There's nothing to tell." I am torn between wishing I had a good story that would make them open their eyes wider and wishing Lizzie had been a heavy sleeper so I wouldn't be in this mess.

Mrs. Cranby is late, but now she comes in with Marylou. Marylou smirks and sits down in the chair next to Lizzie. Mrs. Cranby has her mouth set in an expression that can only be called grim, as if she has just realized that the last year of teaching the thirteen-year-old girls' Sunday school lessons has been a complete waste of her breath.

Not wanting to waste any more breath, she starts right

into the lesson about some wicked cities back in Bible times called Sodom and Gomorrah where the people had taken to idol-worship in a big way and forgotten about God. After they ignored the prophet God sent, God just gave up and decided the best thing would be to just destroy the cities, but he gave a few people who hadn't worshiped idols a warning to pack up and go. And when they left, he said in no uncertain terms not to look back. Mrs. Cranby gives me the eye in this part of the story, as if she knows I'd be the one to turn and look back. She says, "One of the women, Lot's wife, was willful and didn't know enough to mind what she'd been told. She turned around and took one look."

Mrs. Cranby pauses right here, knowing she's got us listening now.

"Well, what happened was this. She turned into a pillar of salt. Just like that." Mrs. Cranby snaps her fingers sharp and fast, and all the while her eyes burn into me. Mrs. Cranby, like Jake, has the air of conviction in her voice, and there is no doubt in my mind that it happened just like she said. I figure I am salt.

After class I am afraid Mrs. Cranby is going to ask me to stay so she can talk to me, but she doesn't. She seems to want to leave as much as I do. She moves down the hall like a battleship, sweeping small children out of her way.

I go to sit down in the church on a long wooden pew where no one will ask me questions I can't answer. Marylou, the last person who I would expect to speak to me, comes up. She says, "You are in trouble now. Just like your sister."

I look straight ahead as if I haven't heard Marylou. People are filing into church now, just like they do every Sunday. I open my Bible and pretend to read. Lizzie told Marylou, and Marylou told Mrs. Cranby. Probably Mrs. Cranby is talking to Mama and Daddy right now. So Marylou is right about me being in trouble. More trouble than I want to think about. But Marylou is just plain wrong about Adra being in trouble. If Adra was in trouble, I would know. Adra left so she could start her life again and forget about Ben. I wonder if Adra was like Lot's wife and looked back.

The sermon goes on and on, and I can't follow it. It's just words like water running. If I were salt, I'd dissolve in water. Instead of imagining I'm salt, I need to imagine I'm more like a big rock you find on the mountain. Hard and sharp and impossible to move.

No one talks on the way home from church. You might think we'd just been to a funeral. One day a long time from now I guess none of this will matter, only now it seems this day will just go on and on, and things are getting worse by the minute. I feel like I'm going to be sick.

When we get home, Daddy says, "You all go in. Except for Cassie."

Jake slides out and slinks into the house without a glance back. Mama goes in, but she looks at me with an expression that is both disappointed and worried, so I know Mrs. Cranby has told Lizzie's story to the both of them.

"I guess you know what Mrs. Cranby told me."

I nod.

"I expect you are old enough to tell right from wrong."

This has never been particularly hard, not like the math problems we have to do in school.

"I guess so."

"Well, when you do wrong you get punished. You are not too old for a whipping. Go get a switch and wait for me in the backyard."

I walk slowly, and my stomach churns, but I expect it isn't just because I'm hungry. Now I need more than anything to be rock and not salt. I cannot dissolve.

I find a switch and wait.

Daddy has taken off his coat and comes out the back door. He wipes his forehead with a handkerchief and puts it back in his pocket.

The first touch of the switch is the worst. It's the surprise. I grit my teeth and try not to cry.

My legs feel like they're on fire, but I'm not going to give in. I wipe the tears past my eyes and take a long breath, letting it out slowly.

Jake comes running out. "Wait, Daddy. Stop! Lizzie

thought she saw Cassie, but it was me. I was out there with Jan. I was trying to get him to fight."

Daddy stands there holding the switch high in the air, looking at Jake. Jake's black eye provides the evidence, and the conviction in his voice finishes the job.

The next thing I know, my legs aren't holding me up, I am dissolving, just falling down—looking up at the bluest sky.

Jake tells me later when I wake up that I passed out. He says it's lucky I did, since I took all Mama and Daddy's attention and they forgot about him. What is amazing is that Jake thinks I was taking punishment for him. The only reason he was going to allow this, he said, was that he thought Daddy would go easy since I'm a girl. But when he saw how hard I was getting switched, he couldn't stand it. He still has no idea I followed him. And Daddy is convinced that Lizzie Miller tells lies just to get attention. I heard him say so to Mama. He says Lizzie Miller could do with a good whipping.

Later Mama comes in my room and sits down on the bed. I'm lying on my side, so the back of my legs don't touch the covers, the way I would if I'd gotten sunburned.

"How are you feeling?" Mama asks, putting her hand on my forehead as if I'm sick.

"I'm all right."

"I am sorry—" She stops, as if uncertain what to say.

"I'm okay." I've never yet heard of anyone's parents apologizing for a whipping before. It's a common belief that most children could do with a good spanking on a regular basis so they won't turn out spoiled. And even though Jake has claimed it was him in the alley and not me, they'd have been asking me questions if I hadn't fainted. I figure that fainting was a blessing.

"I've been meaning to talk with you, and I'd better not put it off any longer. You're growing up fast. Any day now you'll begin to have monthly periods."

This isn't news. Some of the girls at school have already had theirs, and they complain and act as if they are more grown up on account of this. Lizzie calls it the curse, but I can't figure what the fuss is about.

Mama looks out the window, and then she goes on. "Boys change too. They start taking notice of girls. I expect pretty soon, you'll be interested in boys."

I stare at the ceiling, wondering where all this is leading. Am I in trouble after all?

"I am not particularly interested in boys," I say.

"Boys sometimes try to hug and kiss a girl, and this can lead to trouble. It's up to the girl to stop things before they go too far."

I close my eyes and consider the words "too far"—what does this mean exactly?—someplace far away, clear to the ocean, maybe. If you go too far, do you find your way back?

"Tom mentioned he saw you downtown with a boy," Mama says, bringing me right back to the here and now. What is Tom doing, acting like a tattletale? Now that he's married and moved away from home, he's joined the side of the grown-ups.

I open my eyes, look straight at Mama, and say, "That was Jan. He's a friend of mine from school."

"Is that the boy Lizzie claimed she saw you with last night?"

I nod.

"Cassie, a girl has got a reputation to think about. Boys don't have to be concerned as much as girls do. They are expected to sow wild oats. It's different with girls. It's the girl who winds up pregnant."

I take this in and turn it over in my mind. Boys get wild oats. Girls wind up with babies. There is no advantage I can see in having been born a girl. Boys can do what they want, and girls have to pay.

Mama stares out the window, down past the railroad tracks, and I wonder if she's thinking about Adra.

Mama turns back to me, and her expression has changed. It's like she borrowed this look from someone like Mrs. Cranby. She says, "The thing about reputations is they can be destroyed by gossip. It doesn't matter if it's the truth or not. Once a story gets passed around, people take it as fact."

So people are stupid, I think. Why should that rule my

life? If you know a thing is true, that should be enough. What someone else thinks should not matter one bit.

"Did Adra leave because of people talking about her?"

"It didn't help matters any, but I don't think that's the reason she left. She couldn't get over Ben's death. When something like that happens, sometimes a person thinks there's something they could have done, and they blame themselves."

"Why do you think he did it? Killed himself."

"I don't think it's possible to know what was in Ben's mind. I believe Ben was troubled. Sometimes when you're young, you take things so hard that you just think you can't bear it."

Mama sighs and looks out the window, and I wonder if she's remembering being young. She says, "You can't always understand exactly how someone else feels or how troubled they are. Not until it's too late." Mama straightens the quilt on the bed. She stands up.

"One thing, though, it's not too late to keep you from trouble. There's some things you just can't do. You are getting too old to be running all over creation by yourself. I'd like you to come straight home from school and not go wandering off on your own or with anyone." Her voice has this inner core of hardness, as if she's not going to listen to arguments. Now I know what all this was leading to—punishment worse than a whipping.

"That's not fair."

"I am afraid that life is just not fair," Mama says, standing up, closing the subject.

Later I hear people coming in the door. It's Tom and Lula and Aunt Opal. I don't feel like being sociable today, but I'm tired of staying in my room. I go downstairs and into the kitchen. I can hear them all talking, while I pour a glass of milk from the pitcher in the icebox. I expect they all know I got a whipping today and probably have heard the entire story by now. If ever I have children, I will respect their privacy and not interfere in their lives. Unless they fall in the river, in which case I'll pull them out.

I stand in the hallway listening, wondering if they have been talking about me.

Tom is saying, "I've heard some of the men in town talking about joining the Klan. Costs ten dollars."

"That's a good bit of money for folks around here."

Tom says, "Some fellow from out of town wanted to put a leaflet up in the store. I told him I didn't have a place to hang it."

"Good business to stay out of it," Daddy says.

"Robert Morgan's aiming to join. He's been talking some crazy talk against foreigners. He acts as if there's going to be another war, and anyone who's moved here from someplace else is going to be a traitor."

"It's too bad he doesn't have to work for a living. Man has too much time on his hands," Daddy says.

I wonder if work can keep a person from being crazy. I hear all the time that idle hands are the tools of the devil. It sounds as if the devil is just looking for people with time on their hands, instead of working folks. I expect he isn't choosy. And the whole business of craziness—I reckon it comes to some people and not to others for reasons no one knows. It must be something in the way a person's made. Some folks have a gift, like Jan for music. Maybe some are cursed with being not exactly right—like Ben's mother, or like Robert Morgan. And girls are born with a curse that comes once a month, while boys are naturally blessed. Mama is right, life isn't fair.

All week long I come straight home after school and help Mama. I don't think Mama guesses I'm feeling cooped up like a wild bird that's been caught and put in a cage where it looks out at the sky and dreams about flying. I know it won't do any good to argue. Arguing sometimes just makes a bad situation worse.

Eventually, though, Mama will let up on worrying, and things will get back to normal. I come home from school and find Mama ironing the same thing over and over, using so much starch on Daddy's shirts they can almost stand up by themselves. Though I know Mama gave me a talking-to Sunday afternoon, I don't think she is worried on account of me.

On Friday afternoon I come home and find Mama sitting at the kitchen table with Tom, which is unusual, since Tom is generally working this time of the day.

Mama says, "We've had a letter from Adra. Tom brought it home."

"Where is she? Can I see the letter?" I have been waiting for her to write for so long, and I want to see her handwriting, not just hear what she has to say from Mama.

"She's in New Orleans," Tom says. "Lord knows why."

"Tom!" Mama says, sounding exasperated, which she never is with Tom, who Mama thinks is near perfect.

Mama says, "Adra's found a job in a dress shop, and she's thinking about going to this women's college they have there. She always wanted to go on with her schooling."

"There's colleges closer than off in New Orleans," Tom says.

Mama sighs. "New Orleans is a long way."

Tom changes his tone, which has been critical of Adra, saying, "It's not so far. You could take the train and be there tomorrow."

"I guess so," Mama says.

"I didn't know Adra wanted to go to college. I thought she wanted to marry Ben," I say.

Tom says, "Adra would have hated living on that farm with Ben and his mama. I can't imagine they would ever have gotten married. Ben was—" Tom stops, as if he's about to say something he shouldn't, and then goes on, "not ready to get married. And I doubt Adra knew what she wanted. She has certainly put Mama and Daddy through the wringer."

Tom is referring to Mama's Aladdin Washing Machine, which has a wringer you run the clothes through to get the water out.

"Now, Tom," Mama says, "Adra had an awful time dealing with that boy's death. You can't expect her to just go on with her life after something like that happens."

Tom says, "Worse things have happened and people do go on, Mama, without upsetting their families. Sometimes I think that girl is just plain selfish."

Tom sounds just like Aunt Opal. Maybe it comes from living next door to her.

"No, she's not," I tell Tom. "She's just trying to find her own way."

Tom says, "Adra has a cheering section, looks like. I've got to get back to the store. Lula and I'll stop by later."

"Can I see Adra's letter?" I ask Mama, who has forgotten I asked. She takes the letter out of her apron pocket and hands it to me, holding it as if it is something valuable, which I guess it is. Right now it's all we have of Adra.

Adra's handwriting has to be looked at closely, because she writes as if she's afraid of using up too much paper. Even so, it looks nice on the page. I read the letter twice and memorize her address before I hand the letter back to Mama, who folds it carefully and puts it back in her apron pocket.

Adra sounds like she's getting along fine. She writes all about what New Orleans is like and how there're flowers growing even though it's nearly winter. People in New Orleans, she says, talk with a strange accent that sounds foreign to her. She doesn't say anything about why she left the way she did and doesn't apologize for worrying Mama and Daddy. I wonder if she still thinks about Ben and wonder why she had to go so far away. New Orleans must be nearly five hundred miles.

Even after we hear from Adra, Mama seems worried and on edge. It seems like her mind is wandering, and wherever it takes her, it does not make her happy. Last week she ironed everything twice, and this week she has forgotten to iron at all, so I set up the ironing board in the kitchen while Mama sits and stares out the back window. Sometimes I dust, since there is dust settling on the furniture like it's come to stay awhile.

I wish Adra were here. Tom is too busy with Lula just now to be noticing that Mama is on edge. I can't guess what Daddy thinks, except he's none too happy about wearing shirts that I've ironed and which don't come up to his expectations.

Mama doesn't even perk up when Aunt Opal comes to call. Aunt Opal crochets and talks, while Mama listens. Mama's lack of conversation doesn't bother Aunt Opal, who can talk enough for two people.

One afternoon we are all in the kitchen, where I'm peeling potatoes for supper.

Aunt Opal says, "Cassie has turned out to be a big help to you, now she's given up running all over town with her shirttail out."

Aunt Opal is good at saying something nice while saying something you don't like at the same time.

Mama sips her tea and leaves the talking to Aunt Opal.

"Girls should stay home and help their mothers until they get married," she says.

"What if they don't want to get married?" I ask.

Aunt Opal sniffs down her nose. "Your sister would be a sight better off at home helping your mama than living off in that city all by herself. It's not right. 'Sides that, it isn't safe. There's white slavers, and she's got no one to look after her."

Mama has a worried look, so I say, "Adra is just fine. She can look out for herself."

"You are too young to know the first thing about the world. It is a wicked place."

Aunt Opal has lived here in Prosper her whole life, and I don't think she knows any more than I do about the world beyond Prosper, Arkansas. Everyone thinks New

Orleans is just the capital city of wickedness, the nearest thing to Sodom and Gomorrah since Bible times.

Somehow I'm in a mood where I want to answer back to Aunt Opal, and Mama isn't paying the least attention, so I say, "I do too know about the world. I've read lots of books."

"Books. Hmmmmmph! You'd do better to read your Bible."

"Well, we studied about Sodom and Gommorah in Sunday school, so I guess I've read about wickedness."

"Stop being so pert. You are a child. Adra has no business living in a place full of speakeasies and who knows what all. God could destroy New Orleans any day it suits him."

"I haven't heard or seen anything in the newspaper lately about God destroying cities, Aunt Opal."

If Mama were paying attention, she'd have been on me by now and told me to speak politely to my elders, but she's looking out the window way past us.

Aunt Opal raises her crocheting needle and points at me. The yarn is pulled tight so it looks as if it could break. She says, "You don't know the mind of God, young lady."

I don't have an answer to that, and besides I don't want to make Aunt Opal so mad she breaks her yarn, so I let her have the last word.

I figure both Aunt Opal and I have been trying to get

Mama's attention, but our words just wash over her. I put the potatoes on the iron stove and settle down to snap some peas in a pan. Eventually Mama will come back to us just enough to get dinner fixed, which she has been doing for so long it doesn't occupy her at all, so that her movements are as sure and quick and as mindless as Aunt Opal's crochet stitches.

Eight

❧

Mr. *Adams*, the algebra teacher, is tall and has a long scrawny neck that makes me think of an old rooster—a mean old rooster that would peck you if he had the chance. Mr. Adams stalks back and forth in front of the blackboard, beating his ruler against his palm while he talks. No one acts up in his class. Not even Jake, who's taking algebra for the second time and not finding it any easier than he did the first time. Jake sits right near the front of the class, hoping this will help, but so far it doesn't seem to. Cal sits next to him, trying to distract him when Mr. Adams isn't looking. Only mostly Mr. Adams keeps his eyes on us, as if anyone dared to cause trouble.

Mr. Adams raises his ruler, pointing at a problem on the blackboard, and wields the ruler as if it were a sword so it seems he's preparing to battle an army. If anyone makes a mistake up at the blackboard, he'll rap their knuckles. Back in medieval times they had all kinds of torturing equipment—racks and things—Mr. Adams only has his ruler. He is probably sorry he missed the Spanish Inquisition.

Mr. Adams stands at the front, and we all wait to see who he's going to call to the blackboard. I keep my eyes fixed on my algebra book, hoping he doesn't call on me.

Mr. Adams says, "Jake, come up to the board. Let's see what you can do with this problem."

Jake sighs and walks up to the board. I know he hasn't a hope. When Jake does math homework, he pulls his hair and tears up paper, and it never seems to come out right. Jake begins writing, trying to add all the numbers together, but it's not coming out right. He stares at the numbers as if he wishes they'd grow legs and run clear off the blackboard.

"Stop wasting our time. You evidently have not done your homework." Mr. Adams raps the board, catching Jake's fingers so he drops the chalk.

Jake picks up the chalk and walks back to his desk, looking down so it's hard to tell if he's furious or relieved at getting to go back to his seat. I figure he's both. Then I catch a glimpse of his face, and he has this sort of blank look, as if he's just withdrawn and gone someplace inside himself.

Mr. Adams eyes us in the same way a fisherman might

eyeball a can of fat worms, wondering which one he is going to choose to bait his hook.

Cal reaches over to hand Jake a stick of gum, I guess in sympathy. Cal is such a strange friend of Jake's. Sometimes they fight, and other times you'd think they were brothers. The movement attracts Mr. Adams's attention the same way a movement might attract a snake ready to attack.

He snaps, "Cal, maybe you'd like to show us where Jake failed."

Cal wears a perpetual sneer. I expect if God appeared to Cal in a burning bush the way he did to Moses, Cal would sneer and say, "So what, you think I've never seen a burning bush before?" Cal doesn't act a bit afraid of Mr. Adams, but kind of swaggers up to the blackboard. He takes the chalk and with a flourish begins writing numbers at random. Cal doesn't care what x equals—he's filling up the blackboard with numbers.

Mr. Adams beats the ruler against his hand, like the roll of a drumbeat. You can hear the sound of giggling, and the grating of chalk on the board. Mr. Adams doesn't wait for Cal to finish writing but brings the ruler down hard on Cal's fingers.

"You are making a mockery of this class."

Cal pulls back his hand and rubs his fingers in surprise. Then he does something that surprises us all. He grabs the ruler and pulls it away from Mr. Adams and breaks it as easily as a twig. He throws the jagged pieces down.

Mr. Adams's face has turned watermelon red. He strikes Cal with the back of his hand, leaving a red mark on Cal's face. Then he grabs Cal by his shirt collar and his neck and shoves him toward the door. He sputters, "Get out of my class."

He pounds his fist into his hand, not having the ruler. He gives us a stone-cold look, as if we are worms that could turn and bite the fisherman.

I look out the window and can see Cal trudging off. Cal picks up a rock and throws it at the school building, but it falls short.

Mr. Adams picks up his broken ruler and says, "If I hear a peep out of any one of you, you will regret it. You will begin your homework on page seventy-three and do it quietly."

It's so quiet you can hear the pages turning. It's hard to keep silent. I am afraid I might cough. I wish the bell would ring.

Minutes pass by and no one makes a sound. Then Jake drops his pencil. It rolls under Cal's empty desk. Mr. Adams looms over Jake raising the broken ruler. Then someone in the back coughs. It's Jan who seems to be having a coughing fit.

"Stop that coughing right now." Mr. Adams turns away from Jake and steps toward the back of the class.

Jan coughs one more time, then raises his head and looks directly at Mr. Adams with a blank expression and says, "Sorry, something caught in my throat."

Jake picks up his pencil and begins writing furiously. Mr. Adams has no patience with Jake at the best of times, and just now, any movement on Jake's part is suspect.

When the bell rings, the entire class moves toward the door as quick as if someone called "fire." No one wants to be left alone in the room with Mr. Adams.

At lunch Jan and I eat our sack lunches out under the oak tree. Ever since the Saturday when Jan kissed me, we've been eating lunch together and Jake hasn't bothered us. I think when I took that whipping and didn't mention Jake was out in the alley, he changed how he thought about me. I guess he figures if I am grown up enough to take a whipping, I can choose my own friends. I told Jan about the whipping and how I have to stay home after school and help Mama. He felt so bad, I almost wish I hadn't told him. I didn't tell anyone else, though. It's embarrassing to get a whipping when you are thirteen years old, but Jan is always on my side.

Jan opens the wax paper around his sausage and biscuits and says, "It is too bad about Cal. I wonder what will happen to him."

Cal has never been anything but awful to Jan, so I am surprised Jan would care what happened to Cal. I can't always figure Jan out. Sometimes he seems too good to be true. I have never known anyone who actually turned the other cheek, like you are supposed to. I wonder what Jan's secret is.

I answer, "I guess they'll call his daddy, only I don't think he cares much about whether Cal goes to school or not." I remember how Cal threw a rock at Jan and ask, "Were you angry with Cal when he hit you with a rock that night?"

"For a moment. I was glad when your brother jumped on him," Jan says. "When I am angry I hold it as tight as I can, for there is so much to lose. We are new here, and I want to make friends, not enemies."

I remember how Jan gripped the shovel tight, while looking so calm. I wish I could keep my temper sometimes. I guess that's one of the differences between Jan and me.

"Why did you distract Mr. Adams today by coughing so Jake wouldn't get into trouble?" I ask.

"I want Jake to like me, so he will not cause trouble for you. I am happy since we are friends," Jan says, as if this is as simple a fact as two and two make four, though it amazes me that Jan likes me enough to risk getting into trouble in math class.

"If Mr. Adams hit you with the ruler, what would you do?" I ask, teasing.

"I would wish Mr. Adams did not feel it necessary to use the ruler," Jan says.

"Mr. Adams has been hitting students with a ruler

since before we were born," I tell Jan. "Most of our parents had him for math, and think if they put up with it, we can too."

"Your brother Jake would learn better if he were not afraid," Jan says, taking a bite out of his biscuit.

"Jake isn't scared of anything," I say. Jake would never react the way Cal did, but that's not because Jake is afraid. Cal just doesn't have a lick of sense, and Jake does.

Jan says, "When we first came to this country, my family, we did not know but a few words of English. I had a book I studied all the time—even though I did not know what the words meant. I know how Jake feels when he can't work an algebra problem. You should not be punished for making mistakes."

I look across the schoolground to the town. You can see the church steeple rising above the roof of the houses. It seems to me you always get punished for mistakes—that's how it is. It's right in the Bible—you reap what you sow. The sins of the fathers fall on the children. Look what happened to Adam—he took a bite of the apple, and after that there was no Garden of Eden but a vale of tears. That's life. Mr. Adams and his ruler, that's just a small punishment in the scheme of things. If you work an algebra problem wrong, you get a rap on the knuckles. What happens if you do something really wrong, like my daddy kissing the preacher's wife?—a sin called adultery—well, I just don't know what happens. And I don't want to find out.

After school Jake walks home with me instead of walking with his friends. He kicks a rock so it skitters across the road.

"It's too bad about Cal," I say, trying to break through Jake's bad mood, which is like dark clouds ready to break into a thunderstorm.

Jake says, "If I was Cal, I'd just run off and not come back. He's got my lucky rabbit's foot. It sure hasn't brought him much luck."

I figure a whole pocketful of rabbits' feet wouldn't help Cal, but it looks like Jake feels so bad about Cal being in trouble, I'm not going to say so.

The house is so quiet when we go in, you'd think no one lived there. I guess Mama is resting or maybe gone visiting. Jake throws down his books and goes into the kitchen and makes a sandwich with butter and Aunt Opal's preserves. He says, "I think I'd better go look for Cal."

I wish Jake wouldn't go looking for Cal. Since Cal broke that ruler today, I expect he's liable to break anything else that comes his way. He probably figures he doesn't have much to lose.

"I'm coming with you," I say, even though I know I'm supposed to stay home after school. Ever since the time I got the whipping, they've had one set of rules for me and another for Jake. But Jake's in such a strange mood, I figure I'd better stick with him.

"You'd just be in the way," Jake says. He doesn't remember I'm supposed to stay home after school.

"No, I wouldn't. I could help you look."

"All right, come on, then." Jake heads out the kitchen door. "You'll be more help than Cary and Wayne—they've had it with Cal. They think he's gone crazy, the way he acted in class today."

"Why do you think he did it, broke Mr. Adams's ruler?" I ask.

"I don't blame him any. Sometimes I wish I had gumption like Cal. And anyway, even if he acts crazy, you don't quit on a friend."

"Even someone as hard to be friends with as Cal?" I ask, thinking how it's only been a few weeks since Cal gave Jake a black eye.

"That don't matter."

Jake walks fast, like he knows where he's going, following the road north just out of town, which goes to the lake. The lake is about a mile from town down a dirt road. It's a pretty big lake where you can fish, but I don't go swimming on account of water moccasins. Sometimes you can see one slipping through the water on a sunny day, or curled up on a flat rock that's still warm from the heat of the day. There's a high wall on one side of the lake, and that's where we find Cal, perched on top of the wall and drinking from a glass jug. His feet are bare, dangling over the water. The other side of the wall is a sheer drop to a stone floor, and if you were to fall, you could get killed quick.

Cal wipes his mouth with his hand before he calls Jake to come over.

"Wait here," Jake says, but he didn't need to tell me to wait. There is no way I'd walk out on that wall, though it must be nearly two feet wide. It's just too high up for me to feel comfortable. Jake has never been scared of heights. There's not much except algebra that scares Jake.

Jake walks out to where Cal is sitting and settles down next to him. Cal hands Jake the jug, but Jake glances once in my direction and hands it back. They talk for a little bit, then Jake stands up. Cal has a hard time getting up, as if his legs are wobbly. Jake grabs his arm to keep him from falling. I hold my breath as they walk back. Jake has a hold of Cal's arm, and Cal is weaving as he walks. Finally they reach the end of the wall, and I can breathe again. It's then that Cal tumbles down, pulling Jake with him, rolling down the hill to the lake's edge. Cal is laughing, and it's then I realize he's been drinking whiskey from that jug. I've never seen anyone drunk before, though I have heard so much about the evils of drink, I could preach a sermon about it. Jake is frowning, and I guess he might have been worried they'd fall off the wall. The way Cal is laughing so that he doesn't seem afraid of anything, I guess I can't blame him so much, now Jake is safe. If I were Cal, I would go as far away from things as I could, and it looks as if drinking whiskey has taken him so far he's forgotten what happened at school today.

"Come on, Cal, let's get you home," Jake says.

"You go home. I'll stay here."

"You can't stay here. It gets cold at night."

"This will keep me warm." Cal lifts the jug.

"Alcohol thins your blood. You only imagine it keeps you warm," Jake says. "Where'd you come by that bottle, anyway?"

"Bought it off some fellow who stopped for gas at the filling station. He had a whole bunch of bottles hidden in the boot of his car."

"Come on," Jake says, shaking his head at Cal. Then he takes Cal's arm and winds it around his shoulder, helping him walk. Cal walks unsteadier than a toddler who's just finding his feet, so I go to help Jake, taking Cal's other arm. I am shorter than Jake, and our shadows fall before us as we walk—Jake's long and thin, Cal's thicker, and mine just plain short. Our shadows weave before us, and I watch the shapes grow longer as we keep walking the mile or so back to town.

Cal says, "Sweet little Cassie, come to find me before I drown myself."

Cal is not sounding like himself. He's never called anyone sweet before as long as I can remember.

"Don't mind him, Cassie," Jake says. "It's the drink."

Cal begins singing, and I am surprised at how good he

can sing, considering he can't walk straight. We go along like this for a while and then Cal stops singing, and says, "Oh no—" and bends over sick as a dog that's got into something it shouldn't have. A pool of brown liquid forms on the ground, and when Cal stands up, his face has lost all its color. I turn away so as not to embarrass him.

I decide right then I won't be tempted to drink whiskey. Cal's face is dead white, with a red mark where Mr. Adams hit him, and he looks like he might be sick again.

Since Lula is going to have a baby, she's been sick pretty often, and she says it's just part of having a baby. She says it's worth it. Poor Cal is sick for no good reason.

After a little while Cal is better, and Jake and I take up the burden, Cal, and begin walking. Cal can walk a little better now, though it's still slow going.

"I might kill him," Cal says. I guess Cal has finally remembered Mr. Adams hitting him and throwing him out of class.

"You're not going to kill anyone," Jake says.

By the time we reach town, Cal is sicker and barely able to walk. He's heavy for Jake and me to carry. There's no one about, and then I see Jan coming down the street.

"Let me help," he says, and takes my place, sliding Cal's arm around his shoulder and taking some of the burden off Jake.

Jake says, "Thanks. We're trying to get him home—it's close to a mile on the other side of town."

Cal is pretty much a deadweight now, as if he is half asleep. His feet sort of tumble along but don't carry his weight.

Jake says, "Thanks for coughing when you did today. Old Adams was out for blood. You took a chance, he might have gone after you."

"It was too far for him to walk all the way to the back of the room," Jan says, then more quietly to me, "I thought you were to stay home. Will you get into trouble?"

"Not if I'm lucky," I say, figuring sometimes Mama just doesn't notice whether I'm there or not. Besides, I don't want Jan to worry about me.

Cal lives in a small house that hasn't been painted in years. You can see the bare wood where the paint has peeled. Weeds grow long and scraggly all around the house, and over a rusted wagon wheel. The house is dark, and when Jake opens the door, I can't help but wrinkle my nose at the musty smell, like unwashed socks. Jake helps Cal over to a chair.

Cal's daddy comes in from the back of the house. He is gaunt looking so his clothes hang on him sort of like a scarecrow. He says, "What's wrong with my boy?"

Cal lifts his head and says, "I broke it good and proper. He won't use it anymore."

Cal's daddy sniffs, his nostrils twitching. "Have you been drinking? Did you boys get him drunk?" The way he says this, it's not a question but a foregone conclusion.

Jake stands up and says calmly, "I found Cal with a bottle. I threw it away, and we brought him home on account of he was feeling sick."

Cal's daddy says, "What's that foreign boy doing here? Cal wouldn't take up with foreigners."

Jake says, "Jan offered to help us bring Cal home, is all. He's a friend of mine and Cassie's."

"Getting my boy drunk, go on with you, get out."

Cal's daddy watches us leave, as if we might try and steal that old rusted wagon wheel, and Jan takes my arm to guide me through the cluttered yard.

Jake shakes his head. "I'm sorry about that," he says to Jan.

"There is no reason for you to be sorry," Jan says. Then he adds, "It looks like Cal needs the doctor. I'll stop by Dr. Jones's house on the way home."

Jake says, "That would be good."

Jan lifts his hand in a farewell gesture. He dashes off, running lightly as if he's running on air, moving gracefully and quick as wind.

Jake and I walk on. Jake says, "Once when I was talking with Cal, I was boasting what I'd do with old Adams's ruler. I expect that's where Cal got the idea."

"It'll come out all right," I say, hoping it is so. I can tell Jake is still worried.

It's growing darker, and the wind is rustling tree branches overhead. You can feel the dampness in the air that tells you rain is coming. If Jake hadn't gone looking for Cal and brought him home, Cal might have fallen asleep somewhere and wound up with pneumonia. I don't think he'd freeze, though. It's not cold enough.

"Daddy won't like us being late," Jake says, walking faster.

I try and keep up with Jake, figuring I'm in more trouble than Jake. We cut through town. In the store windows everything is dark. The bank stands on the corner, and when we reach it I can see there's still a light on.

"We may be in luck," Jake says, peering through the plate-glass window. "I think Daddy is working late."

I can't see anyone through the window, but Daddy's office is in the back. Sometimes he stays late, and I imagine he counts money or checks figures. Sometimes I think of him counting money like old Silas Marner, who was this person we read about in English class. He didn't have any friends and loved to count his gold coins one by one. Only Daddy has us and Mama, and I guess the preacher's wife.

Jake motions for me to come on. He's slowed down, and you can hear our steps on the sidewalk. It's that quiet.

When we reach the road that turns up the hill toward our house, I look back.

That's when I see her. I can just see her shape, not her face. She's wearing a purple dress and a white lace shawl she draws around her shoulders. I don't need to see her face to know her. It's the preacher's wife. If she were to look in this direction, she'd see me, but she doesn't. She ducks into the entrance of the bank and is gone.

Jake is already a few paces up the road. He stops and waits.

"You look like you've seen a ghost."

"I wish I had," I answer, feeling it would be a sight easier to see something that wasn't real. I don't believe ghosts are real—they make good stories, but you can forget a story after it's done, easier than you can forget something you see with your own eyes. I close my eyes and I can see them, the way they were that Sunday morning—the preacher's wife in Daddy's arms, so close together you'd think there wasn't any air between them.

The darkness grows around us as we walk home. First there's twilight, then dusk, then darkness. It's so dark now we don't have any shadows left; they are swallowed up.

Nine

Nan is sitting at the kitchen table with Mama when we get back. I'd completely forgotten she was coming to stay over the weekend, but it sure is lucky, for Mama is never going to fuss at us for being late or for my taking off with Jake, not with company here.

"I'm sorry I wasn't here when you came," I apologize.

"It's okay. I've been having a fine time visiting with your mama," Nan says. "Anyway, I expect you had a good reason for missing your dinner."

Jake explains to Mama about Cal getting into trouble at school and tells Mama how he was worried that Cal would do something foolish and wind up in more trouble. He tells Mama that Cal was feeling sick so we walked him home, without mentioning the fact that Cal's being sick was on account of his drinking an entire jug of whiskey. Jake knows what to leave out of a story when he tells it.

Nan says to Jake, "Your poor friend. He must have been feeling pretty bad after being thrown out of class."

Jake, who has never been overly concerned with truth, says, "He surely was. He felt just awful."

"Cal has never had an easy time," Mama says.

I felt sorry for Cal earlier, but now that everyone seems to think he's had such a hard time, I get impatient. He didn't have to break Mr. Adams's ruler. There's always more than one way to see things. I wish things were exact and certain like they are in algebra, with only one right answer.

Sometimes I wonder about Adra's leaving the way she did. I knew Mama would worry, but I helped Adra pack and didn't say a word. You hold on to a secret and lock it away as if it were safe in a kind of Pandora's box . . . as if away from light and air, it might die.

Jake hangs around while Nan and I wash dishes. I wish he'd go on upstairs so I could talk to Nan on my own.

After a while I leave Nan talking to Jake and go into the parlor to find Mama. After supper, Mama and Daddy sit in the parlor, and on Saturday nights we usually all gather around the radio and listen. Tonight Mama is sitting by herself in near darkness, rocking in the chair she used to rock us in when we were babies. I don't want to wake her if she's fallen asleep. I just want to make sure she's all right. I can't guess what she's thinking, whether she knows about Daddy and the preacher's wife.

"Cassie, did you need something?"

"No, I just came in to see what you were doing. Jake's been hanging around us all night."

"He's at that age."

"What age is that?" I ask.

"He's begun to notice girls."

I don't think this can entirely be blamed on a person's age. Look at my daddy, who's way past the age of noticing girls, and he's done more than notice the preacher's wife, while Mama sits alone listening to the radio in the dark.

"*You are lucky* to have a brother like Jake," Nan says when we go upstairs to my room. "He's very mature."

"Mature sounds dull," I say, wondering what Jake would think of Nan's calling him mature.

"When I get married," Nan says, "I'm going to marry someone like Jake."

"Not me," I answer.

"Well, of course not, he's your brother."

"No, I mean I'm not going to get married. At least not for years and years."

"What will you do instead?"

"I don't know." I try and imagine what it will be like when I am grown up, but I can't imagine anything but right now.

"You could go live with Adra."

"Maybe."

Nan falls asleep faster than I do. I close my eyes, but the day won't end—just goes on in my mind. After a little while I slip out of bed. I figure I can go downstairs into the kitchen and get a glass of milk and read the book I brought home from the school library. Mama is still waiting up for Daddy, so I tiptoe downstairs so she won't hear me. Mama believes children need to go to bed early to get their rest and frowns on staying up late to read a book, but I figure no one is going to bother with me just at the moment.

I light the lamp, pour a glass of milk, and decide it will go better with a piece of Mama's chocolate cake. I open my library book, *Oliver Twist*, which looks to be about a boy who fell among thieves in the city—a long time ago in England. It is certainly unlikely that Adra will fall among thieves in the city of New Orleans. I've gotten settled down to read for a while when I hear the door open. It's Daddy coming back.

"Sarah," he says, and I can hear worry in his voice.

"I thought I'd wait up for you," Mama says, her voice sleepy. I figure grown-ups are the ones who should go to bed early. They tire easily, whereas I could read all night long if they'd let me. I close my book and turn off the lamp. I figure I'd better go back upstairs before they notice me.

Daddy opens the glass door to the parlor and comes into the hallway as if he's going upstairs, but then he changes his mind and goes back into the parlor. With the door open, they can see me if I try and go upstairs.

"Is Jake all right?" Daddy asks. "Is he sick?"

"He ate his supper and has gone to bed. He's fine."

"Thank the Lord. I was afraid. . . . That boy Cal Jake runs around with got hold of some wood alcohol—the doctor's over there and he called the preacher, said something about Jake having brought Cal home."

"Jake and Cassie found him and helped him get home," Mama says.

"There's something else I need to tell you." Daddy pauses. "It's about the preacher's wife."

"You don't need to tell me," Mama says. In a flash I realize Mama already knows, probably has known even before that Sunday morning when I saw Daddy with the preacher's wife. Maybe when you love someone, there's a sense, as sure as your other senses like smell and taste, that lets you know when something has gone wrong.

Daddy goes on, "It was just a flirtation at first. I never meant for it to go as far as it did. I was flattered by the attention of a younger woman. Tonight she'd stopped by the bank, while he was at the church. It was purely an accident running into him. When he saw us coming out of the bank, I could see the shock on his face, as if I'd given him a blow. I had my arm around her, and well—I hadn't thought about what he would feel or you, either—I guess I thought that I could keep it separate from our life. I'm glad to say there wasn't a scene. He told us what happened to Cal, and when I thought what could happen to Jake . . . I realized what I had to lose . . . might have already lost."

Mama doesn't reply right away, and then she says, "Oh, Duncan, you've hurt me so much. It was as if you had gone away . . . ," Mama says, and I can hear the sadness in her voice, as if the loss has become unbearable. "It was right after Adra left. You were so distant, not wanting to talk."

"I felt like I'd failed as a parent, the way Adra behaved. I couldn't control her. The affair was a kind of escape, but that's no excuse. I never meant to hurt you."

"But you did," Mama says. If sadness were a deep well, Mama's voice would be coming from the bottom.

Daddy says, "I am sorry. I'll do anything to make this come right. We'll find a way past this."

Mama says, "I hope so."

"It will be all right," Daddy says over and over, as if by repeating it, he'll make Mama believe him.

I shouldn't be listening. It's too late now for me to go upstairs. I creep back into the shadows in the pantry and wait until they finally go up to bed, and then wait a while longer for good measure before I creep upstairs and into bed. I still can't go to sleep and keep wondering why, if Mama knew all along, she didn't ever say anything. I can't figure out why. I know in church there is all this talk about turning the other cheek and doing good when people harm you, and there is a Bible verse we had to memorize about faith, hope, and charity, charity meaning love, which is supposed to be the most important of the three. I figure Mama has all three going for her.

Maybe it is something like that, or maybe it is that Mama was fearful something worse would happen. The dentist in our town ran off with his neighbor's wife, and people talked about what a scandal it was. Mama would hate people talking about her.

I fall asleep finally and dream I am falling into the sky through the blueness, and there is nothing to hold on to. I reach out, trying to stop myself from falling, but there is only air. Aunt Opal says dreams have meaning, like in the Bible when Joseph had a dream about his brothers bowing to him. Joseph's brothers got mad and sold him into slavery after he told them about his dreams, making it clear when you have dreams you'd better keep them to yourself. Like secrets. Some things are better not told. I can't go back to sleep, so I get out of bed, my bare feet on the cold wood floor, solid under my feet. It's early morning, and everyone's still asleep, even Mama, who is an early riser. I go outside on the porch. The air is sharp, almost biting cold, cutting through the memory of the dream. Off in the distance a rooster crows to wake people up and tell them it's morning and they are all sleepyheads, or that's what I thought when I was younger.

After breakfast, Nan and I walk downtown. Nan doesn't come to town all that often, so she likes to look in the windows of all the shops. We walk slowly, and she peers in every window, curious about everything, even the barbershop where old Mr. Mickey is getting his beard trimmed. The barber has just finished and pulls the sheet off with a flourish that makes me think of a bullfighter shaking a cape to challenge a bull. White hair falls off the sheet onto the floor, which is already littered with all colors of hair. Mr. Mickey lumbers out of the barber chair and comes out of the shop into the bright sunshine, shielding his eyes from the sun.

"You girls going in for a haircut?" Mr. Mickey jokes.

"Not just now," I say.

"Don't let him get hold of that pretty hair." Mr. Mickey lifts one of Nan's braids. "Like spun gold," he says, then lets Nan's braid go and walks across the street without looking to see if anyone's coming.

"Do you know that old man?"

"That's Mr. Mickey. Folks say he's got a still hidden somewhere up in the hills," I tell Nan, deciding not to mention that he is Aunt Opal's brother and almost a relative.

On the way back from town we pass Lizzie's house. Lizzie is sitting in a wicker chair on the front porch and waves for us to come up. I introduce Nan, and then Lizzie says, "Have you heard what happened to Cal?" Lizzie's expression is solemn.

I figure Lizzie heard about Cal being drunk, and I would just as soon not talk about him, so I say, "Who cares about Cal?"

"Well, he died last night," Lizzie announces.

I get this sick feeling at the pit of my stomach and feel just terrible for the way I was talking just now.

"The doctor said it was wood alcohol that killed him. He must have gotten some bad bootleg," Lizzie says.

I remember Daddy telling Mama the doctor said Cal had been drinking wood alcohol, only I didn't know it could kill a person, and I can see Cal clear as daylight offering Jake a drink, remember the way Jake turned back to see me watching him. I wonder whether Jake would have taken a drink if I hadn't been there.

Lizzie says, "Are you all right?"

"I just can't believe it."

"He's in the mortuary," Lizzie gestures, pointing at the funeral home, which is built onto one wing of their house. "I'll show you."

We follow Lizzie across the yard and into the hallway of the funeral home. There are flowers everywhere in vases so it is like a garden. Even the carpet is patterned with flowers and vines, and the air smells as if a bottle of perfume had overturned. There are chairs with velvet cushions on both sides of the hallway. Lizzie opens the door into the room where people come to pay last respects. There's a boy lying in a plain wood coffin, and his face is pale against the red satin lining. I've seen a coffin before at Ben's funeral, but it was closed and not open like this one. The boy lying there is too still, and his face is wiped clean of feelings. He could be anyone at all. All of a sudden I think I am going to be sick and tear out of the room and don't stop until I am in the yard.

"Haven't you seen anyone dead before?" Lizzie asks in a superior way.

I can't answer. It's all I can do to breathe.

Nan says, "Go get her a glass of water," and Lizzie does, which is amazing, since Lizzie is used to being in charge.

I drink the water slowly, letting it trickle down my throat.

"Come on, Cassie, let's go over to Lula's. It's just down the way," Nan says.

At Lula's, Nan opens the screen door, calling, "Lula, it's us."

"Hey, girls," Lula calls, and then she sees my face and says, "Come in and sit down and tell me about it."

Nan tells her about Cal and how Lizzie took us to see his body in the funeral home.

Lula says, "The nerve of that girl taking you in to see him laid out when you'd just heard he was dead."

I can't get the picture of Cal just lying there in that room all by himself out of my mind.

"Lizzie said he'd died of wood alcohol. What does that mean exactly?" Nan asks.

"Sometimes bootleggers use ingredients you wouldn't feed a pig. Folks up in the mountains have been making moonshine for years without killing anyone, but now with prohibition and all there's lots of money in it. Any fool can set up a still and make bootleg whiskey and sell it." Lula's face grows even more serious as she says, "You girls promise me you'll never drink any bootleg—not ever. There's lots of folks got sick from it. Up in Kansas there's people can't walk ever again after drinking bootleg whiskey." Then, remembering Cal, she shakes her head. "That poor boy."

"We'd better go find Jake," I say, getting up to go.

We don't find Jake anywhere and finally go home, but Jake isn't there either. We go in and find Mama in the kitchen, and I tell her about Cal.

"Another boy dying in this town," she says. "It's going to be hard on Cal's daddy. Cal was all he had."

It didn't look to me like Cal's daddy took much care or notice of him, but I know better than to say so to Mama.

"First Ben and now Cal," Mama says.

"Ben didn't die because of drinking whiskey," I say.

Mama wipes her hands on her apron and sits down by us at the table and says, "Ben had been drinking before he died. He might not have walked in front of that train if he had all his senses about him."

This is the first time I've heard that Ben had been drinking. No wonder I never understand things—they never tell me everything they know. Things are kept from children to keep them safe, only it doesn't always work. I never heard about anyone dying from wood alcohol before today.

Jake comes in while we are sitting at the table. His face is pale and drawn, so he looks older than his fourteen years.

"Cal's gone," is all he says.

Mama gets up and puts her arm around Jake's shoulder. She says, "I am very sorry about Cal."

Jake allows Mama to keep her arm around his shoulder for a minute before he pulls away. "I wish I'd have stopped him drinking that stuff. I wasn't able to help him at all."

Mama says, "You were his friend, and you went looking for him when he was in trouble. That was a good thing. He'd have died somewhere all by himself if you all hadn't brought him home."

"It wasn't enough," Jake says.

Jake goes upstairs to his room. After a while I go up to see if he feels like talking. Jake is sitting on the bed and drawing on a sketchpad. His eyes look dark in the glow of the lamplight as he concentrates on the drawing. I stand in the doorway, not wanting to intrude, but hating to leave Jake on his own if he's feeling bad.

"Cassie, either come in or take yourself off somewhere. You're getting on my nerves standing there."

I take a chance on further getting on Jake's nerves and take a seat on the chair in front of Jake's desk. Outside the sky is turning purple-black, like Jake's eye the time Cal hit him, only on a larger scale.

"What are you drawing?" I ask Jake. I know better than to go look over his shoulder.

"Nothing that matters," Jake says.

Jake can draw anything—it just comes natural. I expect it helps him figure out what he's thinking and work things out.

I sit quietly looking out the window. It seems like Jake has forgotten I'm there when he says, "It's just so hard to take in. Yesterday Cal was acting crazy at school, and now he's dead and going to be buried. Pretty soon it will be as if he was never born."

"No, it won't. You'll always remember him."

Jake stops drawing and says, "And if it had been me, what would you all be doing—planning what to wear to my funeral?"

"I wouldn't," I say, indignant.

"Yes, you would. Life goes on. You do whatever comes next."

"Well, I'd never forget you. I wouldn't stop missing you."

Jake says, "I'd have taken a drink sure as shooting if you hadn't been there."

I couldn't stand for anything to happen to Jake. The thought he might have taken a drink scares me so much I try and change the subject, but all I can think is Cal and Ben, and the way they died for no good reason.

"Did you know that Ben had been drinking before he died?" I ask Jake. "Do you think that's why he walked in front of the train?"

Jake's voice is impatient, answering, "Cassie, if everyone who got drunk walked in front of trains, the railroad would be plumb littered with bodies. The trains would never run on time."

"Do you know why he did?"

"How should I know? You ask too many questions."

"How will I ever know anything if I don't ask?"

Jake sighs. "You don't have to know everything."

"I wish I understood why things happen. Adra wouldn't have gone if Ben hadn't died. They'd have got married and lived here like Tom and Lula."

"Ben wouldn't have ever married Adra."

"How do you know?" I feel ready to quarrel with Jake. He always thinks he knows more than me.

"I just happen to know that."

"How?"

"If I tell you, swear never to say a word. Not to Mama or anyone."

"I swear," I say, though I know I'm not supposed to swear.

"The night Ben got killed, some of the high school kids were in the field by the railroad tracks just out of town. Adra and Ben were there. One of the fellows had brought some home brew. Don't look like that. It wasn't poison."

"Since Cal died, the idea of drinking makes me feel sick," I tell Jake.

Jake goes on. "Cal was with me that night. We had stayed over at Cary Black's, but we snuck out after everyone was asleep. You know what they do. No, I guess you don't. . . . Well, some of the couples would go off by themselves in the woods to fool around. I don't think Ben much cared for being there. He was kind of a loner. They were mostly Adra's friends. Ben had been drinking a lot, and I don't think he was used to it. After a while Adra took Ben's hand and led him off down the trail into the woods.

"Cal punched me on the arm and dared me to follow them. I reckoned all they'd be doing is kissing, and I couldn't see any harm in it. Don't you ever tell Adra.

"We were a ways back so they wouldn't hear us, and

when we finally come upon them . . ." Jake stops, as if he's not sure he should be telling me about what he saw.

"Adra was wearing her slip, and Ben was in his long johns. Adra's dress was just hanging there on a bush. I grabbed hold of Cal and tried to get him to leave, but he wouldn't come, and if I'd have fought him, they would have heard us. I was furious at Cal."

I don't know what to think. Jake sometimes doesn't seem to have the sense he was born with, to go with Cal to spy on Adra. I don't think I want to hear any more, but Jake is already talking.

"I never thought they'd be doing . . . I wouldn't have gone after them. Ben had spread his shirt out on the grass like a blanket, and they were lying there kissing when all of a sudden Ben pulled away like Adra was hot as fire and said, 'Don't touch me,' like Adra might burn him. Adra stood there holding his shirt in front of her. He wouldn't hardly look at her and acted like she wasn't there, as if Adra had done something wrong. She was crying, and said Ben had promised. Ben just stood there looking sick, and then he said, 'I'm sorry. I hate myself for the way I am.' Then he just walked off without his clothes. I managed to pull Cal away then. When we were out of hearing distance, Cal called Ben a 'sissy boy.' I just busted loose and fought Cal then, before he could say anything about Adra."

"Jake, I don't know how you could have followed her like that. I'd expect it of Cal, but not you."

I leave Jake's room, wishing I hadn't asked so many questions. I feel sick. I go into Adra's room, which seems emptier now than ever before. I remember Adra saying Ben couldn't bear to touch her, only it must have been he couldn't bear her to touch him, which seems even worse. I keep imagining how it must have been for Adra to have Ben walk away and leave her alone in the darkness.

I'm glad Nan is still visiting. It seems to take the edge off what's happened. Just watching Mama talking with Nan about her family while they put the dishes away, it seems like a normal evening and not like someone we know has died.

"How's Jake?" Mama asks.

"He's resting."

"It's been a shock for him and for you, too." Mama comes over to where I'm standing and rubs my shoulder.

"Don't fuss." I don't want Nan to see me being treated like a child.

"Nan told me about that Lizzie taking the two of you into the funeral home," Mama says. "I can't think what her parents are thinking of, the way they've allowed that child to do whatever comes into her mind."

"Lizzie's all right," I say, since Lizzie's not around to provide her own defense.

Nan says, "There's more than one opinion about that. You just don't see the bad side of people."

"Lizzie's grown up living right by the funeral home, and she's comfortable around dead people. It's just Lizzie, the way she is." Nan hasn't known Lizzie all her life. It's hard to get used to someone like Lizzie all at once.

Later, when it's time to go to bed, I can't go to sleep. I keep imagining Cal the way he was in the funeral home, then when I close my eyes, it's Ben's face I see.

Ten

❧

Cal's funeral is held Sunday afternoon at the graveyard. Mama said Cal's daddy won't set foot in a church,
not even when he married Cal's mother. Jake wears his
best clothes and looks as solemn as the pallbearers who
carry the coffin. Everyone stands in a circle around the
grave, and Preacher Edwards stands beside the coffin,
which is next to the grave. Jake stands between Mama and
Daddy, and though no one is touching him, it seems as if
their being close helps him somehow. Daddy does not
even glance at the preacher's wife standing on the other
side of the grave.

It's a cloudy day, and it seems like the sun is hiding
up in the sky. The grass is turning brown now, the way it
does at the beginning of winter, and with everyone wear-

ing black it seems like the world is turning dark.

Preacher Edwards begins the service, saying, "Cal Turner was a fine young man. He will be missed surely by those who knew and loved him."

He pauses and then says emphatically, "Cal is no longer with us, but we can all rejoice because Cal is with our Lord in heaven." Cal's daddy looks a long way from rejoicing. I expect he'd rather Cal was with him instead of up in heaven with the Lord. Preacher Edwards goes on talking. "We all want the best for our children—for them to grow up without hardship and trouble—but that is not the way in this world. When a young man like Cal dies before his time, it is especially hard. We can't always understand God's plan for us, but know that God has a plan and he is compassionate and forgiving."

I figure Preacher Edwards is trying to offer some comfort, since most people here are acquainted with Cal and figure he will be in sore need of forgiveness.

He goes on talking in a hopeful voice, "We are all children of God—of light, not of the darkness," and looks around the circle of mourners.

I think of how Mama still thinks of Adra as a child, though she's grown now, and how she is always fixing food for Tom just the way she always did when he lived at home. I don't see myself as a child and get annoyed when Mama and Daddy treat me like one, only just now I imagine all of us standing as if we are a circle of children standing in a circle of light while outside the circle the world is turning dark.

Later that afternoon Jake takes his shotgun and goes off into the woods. Mama doesn't stop him, even though he's not supposed to hunt on Sunday.

A few minutes later Daddy calls me into the parlor. I always expect the worst on these occasions.

Daddy says, "Both your mother and I have noticed you have a steadying influence on Jake."

I am too surprised to speak.

"You are no longer confined to barracks, as they say in the army. You've been a great help to your mother, and we are both grateful you decided to go with Jake when he went to find Cal that day," he says.

"I figured Jake was upset by what happened at school, so I stayed with him," I say.

"It was good you did. I know I can count on you to look out for your brother."

It's Jake that Mama and Daddy are worried about now, because of what happened to Cal. I guess there is always one of us they are going to be more worried over than another. It's Jake's turn now.

———

It sure sounds as if Daddy is telling me to be my brother's keeper, only I figure no one could keep Jake. I feel like I let him down the other night when he told me how he and Cal followed Adra. I know he felt bad, only I let my own feelings get in the way. Jake really bothers me sometimes when he does something so dumb. I decide to go look for him. It occurs to me Jake might have stopped by the graveyard to pay his last respects on his own, so I head in that direction.

There's no one in the graveyard, but the preacher's wife is sitting on a bench outside the church.

"Have you seen Jake?" I ask, walking up beside her.

"Not since the funeral," she says. "Is your brother all right?"

"I guess so. He knew Cal ever since he was little, and even though they fought sometimes, Jake liked him."

"Sometimes you miss the people you fight with the most," she says.

"Yes, ma'am," I say, figuring I'd not miss Marylou one bit if anything were to happen to her. Or maybe I would. You get used to people being the way they are, and if they aren't around, maybe it's like an empty place at the table, like Adra's.

"Please don't call me ma'am. It makes me feel old."

"All right," I say, wondering why she would feel old. She can't be all that much older than Adra.

"Of course, you probably think I am old." She laughs. "I can remember when I thought everyone over twenty-five was old."

"Are you twenty-five?" I ask, before I remember my manners.

"Closer to thirty," she admits, "but you won't give me away, will you?"

"I am not a gossip," I say.

"No, I am sure you are not. I'm sorry I didn't get to know your sister, Adra. I am full of admiration for the way she has made a new life in a strange city all on her own. That must take courage," she says.

I'm so surprised by what she's said, I don't reply. The preacher's wife is the first person I've met who doesn't think Adra should have stayed home where she belongs.

"Adra must have had a difficult time coming to a decision about leaving home," she says.

"I guess," I say, not really wanting to talk about Adra, even though she seems sympathetic. I remember the night Adra left, how she seemed angry one minute and sad the next. I expect leaving home is not ever easy, even if you are not sad, the way Adra was.

The preacher's wife looks across the empty graveyard, which seems more desolate now than it did with all the mourners wearing dark clothes. Cal's grave is covered with wreaths of flowers, bright against the brown earth.

"I imagine you must miss your sister," she says. She's

still looking over the graveyard to the trees beyond, which have a few yellow leaves remaining.

"Not so much as I did at first. Adra's going to go to college. I expect I'll go too, once I'm older." This is the first time I've actually come out and said what I might do, but it seems possible.

She says, "I am almost envious of Adra's ability to pick up and leave and begin her life in a new place."

I nod. I wonder if I'm imagining it, but she seems glad of my company. I glance at her face and notice she's not wearing lipstick. She seems paler than usual in her funeral black, and I wonder if she misses seeing my daddy. I am sure that what happened between them has ended.

After a little while the preacher comes out of the church and walks over to the bench.

"Hello, Cassie, how nice of you to keep my wife company while she was waiting on me." Then he turns to her and says, "Are you ready to go, dear?" and his voice is different, polite but cooler somehow.

He doesn't touch her or take her arm, and they walk over to the car without talking.

I've heard Mama say marriage is for better or worse, and from what I can tell worse is just as likely as not. Maybe how a person feels can change directions, like the wind blowing east one day and west the next. It seems like love shouldn't change, though, no matter what. People in families don't stop loving each other even when they are upset when someone does something they don't like. I know Jake wouldn't have followed Adra if he could do it all over again, and I bet Daddy would not have carried on with the preacher's wife if he had been thinking clear.

Eleven

Cal would be surprised if he could hear the way people are talking about him at school on Monday morning. In homeroom Miss Sanders talks about the tragedy of Cal's death. The way she describes him, you'd think she never had him in her class. To hear her tell it, Cal was one of the brightest pupils she'd ever had in her class. She seems to have forgotten all the times he was late for school and how he sometimes talked back.

All day long people talk about Cal in such a way it seems they don't remember him at all—except Marylou, who says, "I don't know why everyone is so upset. No one liked him except Jake Hill." You can pretty much count on Marylou to say something mean.

———

The first thing I notice going into algebra class is that Mr. Adams is standing at the blackboard without his ruler. I glance over at his desk, and as far as I can see he hasn't replaced his ruler.

No one ever comes into algebra class feeling lighthearted, and today is no different. There's no whispering and no giggling. Jake looks as if his mind is miles away. I hope Mr. Adams won't call on him.

Mr. Adams assigns us pages of homework and tells us to begin now. He leaves the room. After a few minutes, when it looks as if he's not coming right back, Lizzie and Marylou begin whispering. One of the boys in the back throws a spitball, and this causes a chain reaction among all the boys except Jake. Jake looks a million miles away.

After school Jake waits outside for me to walk home, so I know he's still feeling low. Cary calls out to him to go with him and Wayne, but Jake acts like he doesn't hear him. Jake trudges along looking at the ground while he walks, and doesn't even look up when Jan catches up to us.

Jan says, "I'm sorry to hear about your friend."

Jake scrutinizes Jan's face before answering, "I don't know as why you'd be sorry. Cal wasn't your friend."

"I know. You will miss him," Jan says, his voice calm, understanding Jake in some way I don't.

Jake nods, and doesn't say anything for a minute or two. Then he says, "I'll kill the fellow who sold him that bootleg if I ever run across him."

Jan doesn't seem alarmed at Jake's statement, but I try and change the subject. I hate for Jan to think my brother has violent tendencies.

I say, "Everyone was saying nice things about Cal today."

Jake snorts. "Bunch of hypocrites." He walks ahead a few paces, and I am worried Jan will think Jake is meaning us, but Jan seems to understand.

Jan says, "Long ago, when my friend died I am very angry. That is how Jake feels."

I am struck by this, for it makes sense. Grief is all mixed up with anger. Jake is ready to snap anyone's head off who's nice to him. And Adra acted mad at the whole world when Ben died.

"He sure isn't acting like himself," I tell Jan, glad he is walking along with us. His calmness just seems to flow over me. It is a mystery to me how Jan seems to know how I'm feeling.

Jake waits a little ways until we catch up, and then walks along beside as if nothing has happened. We walk along without saying much until Jan says, "Last night I heard some men talking outside the filling station about what they'd do to some old man who has a still up in the hills."

Jake says, "Cal didn't buy that stuff from anyone around here. He bought it off some fellow who was passing through. He told me."

"I bet they meant old Mr. Mickey," I add for Jan's sake, since Jake already knows this. He's our aunt Opal's brother, and she is always worrying about the way he lives off by himself."

Jan says, "If you know him, I'd tell him to take care. It is odd, but they were not going to do anything on a Sunday, but they seemed to think it was just fine to go after him on a weekday."

Jake says, "I know where he lives. I've taken groceries there before. It's only a couple miles outside town. We could be there in half an hour."

We leave our books on the front porch instead of going in, avoiding Mama, who might ask us questions. There is a sense of urgency, and Jake leads off running, with Jan and me following close.

Leaving town, Jake cuts through the woods and only slows down when the brush becomes too thick to pass quickly. It's afternoon, but there's not too much light left in late fall, so as we pass through the dense pines it seems as if darkness has fallen. The ground is thick with pine needles, so we don't disturb the silence of the woods. And then we hear voices in the distance. Up ahead there is a flash of white, and then we see them, passing like a company of ghosts, their white sheets stark against the dark green pine trees. They have hoods that come to a long point, as if there is something under them that is not human. I scrunch close to Jake, shivering, and Jan, who is beside me and so very still, takes hold of my hand.

I remember Tom talking about how the Klan was trying to get members in our town. And what he said about them hating people from foreign countries. They form a circle, and one man begins speaking in a ringing voice that carries to us. He sounds like a preacher, but not Preacher Edwards, who has a northern accent. Maybe it is because he is speaking about the wrath of God falling on the wicked. There are slits in his robe for his eyes, and they look pitch-black, like the darkness within a cave in the mountains. It is like something from the scary part of the Bible, the Book of Revelation. The closed circle and shine of white luminous against the dark pines strikes terror in my mind so I can hardly breathe.

Jan's face beside me is pale, and I wonder if he knows the Klan hates people from foreign countries. Jan's hand tightens around mine, while Jake watches with this kind of intent excitement, the same way he'd watch the opposing team if he were playing football.

The man who sounds like a preacher has gone on talking in general terms about how sin is rampant in our town and then about the evils of bootleg whiskey, which has caused death and destruction among us.

Now he calls them to action. "We will destroy the stills that are in these hills and root out evil at its source."

One of the other men says, "Some of those stills are so well hidden the devil himself couldn't find them."

The speaker replies, "No one can hide from the Ku Klux Klan. Those who make moonshine will feel our wrath."

It's clear to me they have somehow come to the conclusion they are bringing down the wrath of God. Jake motions us to leave as someone brings up old Mr. Mickey's name.

When we are out of hearing distance, Jake whispers, "We'd better hurry and warn Mr. Mickey."

We race through the woods and scramble down ravines, sliding in the red dirt. Jan keeps near me and takes my hand to help me over logs.

I am afraid for old Mr. Mickey. People at church call him a backslider because at revivals he gets religion, but he just can't keep it. We reach the cabin where he lives before the Klan. It's made of logs and looks to be as old as Mr. Mickey. The front door is standing open, and Jake runs right inside as if he'd been invited. The inside of the cabin is not as rustic as the outside. The walls are painted, and there is a braided rug in front of the hearth. On the mantel above the fireplace are pictures of people I don't recognize, except there is one of some children, and I'd bet the older girl with a grave expression is Aunt

Opal as a girl. In one picture a younger Mr. Mickey is standing next to a girl who has curls. She's holding his hand and smiling as if she'd just learned something that made her happy. I wonder if she was his wife, though she must have been dead a long time, because I never heard anyone talk about her. Mr. Mickey is slumped in a chair, napping.

Jake says, "Mr. Mickey, wake up!"

Mr. Mickey nods, but he doesn't open his eyes. Maybe his dreams have more hold on him than Jake's voice, for it is not until Jake shakes him that he wakes.

"What's the matter, boy?"

"The Klan is coming to tear down your still, or maybe worse."

"They'll never find it. Government revenuers couldn't find it, I don't figure the Klan will either."

"You don't want to be here when they come," Jake says.

"Where's my shotgun?" Mr. Mickey blinks and looks at the empty gun rack on the wall. Mr. Mickey has a reputation of being absentminded, but he clearly isn't afraid of using his shotgun if he ever finds it. I'm not sure how good his aim would be, since he's peering in corners and hasn't noticed the gun standing by the fireplace.

Jake picks up the gun, which has been gathering cobwebs for a long time. He cleans off the cobwebs. Jake likes guns of all kinds, likes to polish and clean them as well as shoot them.

Jake says, "I'll carry it for you. I think it would be best to leave."

I find a satchel and gather up Mr. Mickey's pictures, just to be on the safe side. Jan takes Mr. Mickey's arm and steers him toward the door.

Mr. Mickey stops on the porch, and I think he's forgotten why we are going, for he says, "Can't go without my fishing pole."

Jan goes back and collects Mr. Mickey's pole and his tackle box. The three of us start down the trail, away from the direction we came so as to not run into the Klan. I guess Jake plans to circle around and take another way back to town.

We are a half a mile down the trail when Mr. Mickey comes to a halt. He says, "I'm not going a step farther without my fishing hat. I never have any luck at all if I leave it behind."

Jake has this exasperated expression on his face, but before he can snap at Mr. Mickey and make him mad, I say, "I'll get it for you."

"Cassie, you can't go back there," Jake says.

"I'll be quick," I say, and I'm off. Jan follows, and I call for him to stay with Jake.

Jan says, as he runs beside me, "I'm not letting you go back there by yourself."

Coming up to Mr. Mickey's cabin, I stop and look

around, but there's no one about so I tear into the house and grab Mr. Mickey's hat, which I noticed earlier hanging from a hook just inside the door.

Jan waits on the porch, listening. "Cassie, hurry, I can hear them."

He pulls me into the bushes a little ways from the house as the men stalk into the yard as if they own it.

One of the men says, "There ain't no still here."

Someone else says, "Could be it's hidden somewheres near here along the creek. Man as old as him can't be troubled to go too far."

"He's not here," the leader announces as he peers through the doorway into the cabin. "Some of you men go search for the still." "You there"—he gestures—"gather up some brush. We're going to show what happens to moonshiners."

Jan takes my hand, and we creep through the woods, careful not to make a sound to draw their attention. I figure we have gotten away when a man wearing robes and a hood steps from behind a tree. I don't think he was with the others, for they haven't had time to reach us.

He grabs my shirt collar and jerks it, saying, "I know you. You're the ones brought my boy home to die." His voice is low and angry.

"You're Cal's daddy," I manage to say in spite of how afraid I am.

"That's right. These robes are plumb useless." He pulls the hood off and his eyes are bloodshot. He wipes sweat off his forehead and pushes his hair back.

Now that I can see his face I am not as terrified as before. He lets go of my collar and moves a step closer to Jan, saying, "Did you give my boy that bottle? How come you and that Jake Hill aren't dead, and my Cal is?"

"Cal told Jake he bought the whiskey from a man who stopped at the filling station. That man had a whole bunch of bottles he was taking somewhere to sell," I say.

"Everybody knows old Mickey has sold moonshine from his still, sometimes to boys," he says.

"I guess so, but he'd been doing that for years and years and never killed anyone," I say, remembering what Lula said. "Bootleggers sometimes use bad ingredients. I bet Mr. Mickey wouldn't use anything that would harm a person."

"You might be right," Cal's daddy says. "You say that Cal told Jake he bought it off someone at the filling station. That wouldn't be old Mickey then. I never heard of Mickey doing business at the filling station."

Cal's daddy throws down the hood and says, "They're burning down the wrong man's house. There's no use in it, no use at all."

Now there's a crackling sound you can hear from Mr. Mickey's house, and smoke seeps through the forest covering us.

Cal's daddy bends his head as if he's just given up, then he shakes his head and raises it and looks straight at Jan and says, "I heard you were the one who went for the doctor. Thank you for your trouble."

I am surprised at his sudden change of manner, but then he says, "Go on now, get out of here before they catch you."

Jan and I set off running, darting through the woods quick as foxes who've heard the bay of the hounds.

Jake and Mr. Mickey are still standing in the same place waiting, and I can see Jake is relieved to see us coming. I hand the hat to Mr. Mickey.

He says, "I thank you." Then he looks at me, as if he's not sure who I am, and says, "Did I promise to take you fishing one day?"

"I don't know that you did, but I'd like to go sometime," I say. It sure seems like Mr. Mickey has forgotten about the Klan coming and thinks we're going on a fishing trip. He settles the hat on his head as if it is his most valuable possession. As he walks down the trail, his steps are jaunty, as if the hat has made him feel younger or maybe more himself, remembering some far-gone year when he promised to take some girl like me on a fishing trip.

———

Jake leads the way, with Mr. Mickey following and Jan and me just behind. After a little while, I catch up to Jake and walk beside him.

Jake says, "Where do you figure we should take him?"

"Aunt Opal's."

Jake asks, "You think she'll let him in her house? She's awfully fussy."

Jake is probably remembering Aunt Opal making him take his boots off before coming in.

"Of course she will. He's her brother. When they were growing up, she looked after him."

"Poor Mr. Mickey," Jake says, and I don't know if he is referring to Mr. Mickey's growing up with Aunt Opal looking after him or his situation at present.

"I'm sorry about what I said the other night—when you told me about following Adra—you didn't mean harm."

Jake looks down the trail. "I shouldn't have told you."

"You felt bad about it is all. And bad about Cal. I let you down, the way I acted."

"No, you didn't," Jake says. After a little he says, "When we get closer to town, I'll go on ahead and tell Tom what happened so he can tell Aunt Opal we're coming."

Jake avoids Aunt Opal when he can, knowing her tendency to fuss at him.

Mr. Mickey must have overheard, for he says, "I'd just

be in Opal's way. I'll stay out in the woods." I figure some-times Mr. Mickey is more aware than I give him credit for.

"No, you won't," Jake says. "She's got lots of room, and she'll be real glad to see you. She told us she practically raised you."

Mr. Mickey goes along with Jake, the way most people do when he suggests something. Jake is good at getting people to do stuff they might not want to do.

Jake runs ahead when we reach town, and we find Tom and Aunt Opal waiting on the porch when we arrive.

Aunt Opal makes a fuss over Mr. Mickey, though she does make him take his boots off before he comes in. She fixes iced tea, and there's apple pie and cream for all of us, so I know she is pleased.

Tom asks, "Did you recognize any of the men?"

Jake says, "Shoot, they were all wearing hoods, and we couldn't get too close to them," as if he is disappointed.

Neither Jan nor I say a word about Cal's daddy. I figure he's got enough trouble, and he wasn't one of the men who were burning up Mr. Mickey's cabin.

Jan says, "There was a man, a stranger, I heard down at the filling station last night talking about an old man with a still."

Tom says, "I can't imagine anyone who lives here would harm Mr. Mickey. That man you saw was probably someone hired by the Klan to come in and stir things up. The three of you did well to bring Mr. Mickey here."

When we leave, Aunt Opal gets Tom to find Mr. Mickey some of his clothes, and I can tell she can't wait to get him cleaned up. She looks happier than I've seen her in a long time. Once in a while someone's misfortune is someone else's good luck, and I expect Aunt Opal will like having someone to cook for and look after, even if it's only for a little while.

Twelve

Tom organizes a log raising to build Mr. Mickey a new house. It used to be that log raisings were pretty common, Daddy says, but I have never been to one. There's lots of people around these parts that know how to go about building a log house, and Tom has not wasted any time getting those folks involved. Everyone is coming and bringing food, and Tom has made sure the Chance brothers are going to come and bring their fiddles for a square dance afterward. They are the best fiddlers in these parts, and when I told Jan about them, his eyes just lit up. I told him he had to bring his violin, that they always welcome another fiddler. Jan isn't a fiddler exactly, but he can play music as good as any I've ever heard.

The day of the log raising, the sun shines, and even

though it's late November, it's warm outside. Tom and Jake have been working the past few weeks skinning the bark off the logs and getting them ready. Some days Jan has come by, and we've gone over to help them. It turns out that Mr. Mickey isn't as poor as I thought he was from the way he lived. He used to farm, and when he sold his farm, he put his money in the bank and forgot about it. He has enough money to buy some land right at the edge of town that backs up against a wooded ridge, so he will feel as if he is living out in the hills but be close so Aunt Opal can look after him when he's forgetful. Tom and Lula bought some land near him and are going to build a house eventually.

We all get up early Saturday morning. Jake and Daddy go over to get started with the work, while Mama and I get the food ready to bring over. Mama has baked pies all week long, and now we are frying chickens and making potato salad, enough for an army.

Mama says, "It has been good for Aunt Opal to have her brother to look after these past few weeks. It's too bad she didn't have a family. She and Wilbur were never able to have children."

"She's got us." I guess she likes us in her own way, though sometimes it's hard to believe.

Aunt Opal has been bossing Mr. Mickey around and keeping him in line these past few weeks. He is always clean and wearing fresh ironed clothes. He doesn't seem to pay too much attention to Aunt Opal's talking, though. I think his mind wanders.

Daddy comes back to drive us over and to help carry the food. As we load up the car, Daddy says, "There's been a good turnout. Tom must have convinced everyone in town to come."

"I knew there would be. Everyone felt bad about Mr. Mickey losing his home," Mama says.

"He'll have a better house now. That cabin of his was dilapidated. It wouldn't have lasted."

"No, I suppose not. Still, it was his."

"He'll like this new place."

"I'm sure he will. Tom has certainly worked hard to get things ready."

"Tom has the knack for organizing people to get a job done," Daddy says. "He'll make something of himself yet. He's been killing time at the store."

I never knew Daddy didn't want Tom to work at the store, that he thought he should be doing something else. He always seems to leave Tom alone to find his own way.

Mama says, "Tom does real well at the store."

Daddy says, "Tom does all right when he puts his mind to it."

Mama says, "And I am sure Adra will get along well at school."

I know this is still a sore subject. Daddy hasn't entirely forgiven Adra for leaving.

"She's smart enough," Daddy says. "But I'll be glad when she settles down."

I know he means when she gets married. Daddy may be forward-thinking in some respects, but he is awfully old-fashioned in thinking women should get married and that should be their whole life.

When we reach the place where Mr. Mickey's new house is going to be, we drive off the road and park in the grass alongside horses and wagons and two other cars. I can see Jan working beside Jake and another boy. They are cutting notches into a log fastened on a sawhorse. The way Tom explained it to me, they cut notches in the wood to hold the logs in place, instead of using nails. Jan looks up and smiles when he sees me. I help Mama with the food and am going over to say hello to Jan when Lizzie calls, "Cassie, come over here."

Lizzie is sitting on a quilt under a tree with two other girls from school. I'm glad Lizzie and I are sort of friends again, even if she's unpredictable. Looking back on things, it seems I felt as if the girls in my class didn't like me much, but it might have been the way I was looking at things. If you are a little different from the group and don't fit right in, you sometimes feel that you aren't liked whether it's a true fact or not.

Lizzie says, "Do you know the boy over working next to your brother and Jan?"

"No, I've never seen him before." I glance over at the

boy she means. He's taller than Jan, and as he wields the ax, you can see the line of muscles in his arm stand out. He glances in our direction as if he knows we are watching him and doesn't care.

"He looks older than us," I tell Lizzie.

"Not really," Lizzie says with a smile, and it dawns on me Lizzie is taken by the way this new boy looks. Lizzie has always gotten everything she wants, but then she has never wanted a boy quite like this one. He looks like he might belong on the screen at the picture show.

Marylou arrives with her family in a wagon, drawn by a mule. There are a whole bunch of children younger than her in her family. She's the oldest one left at home, as her other sisters are all married, and she bosses her little brothers and sisters around, telling them what to do.

She comes over, and Lizzie says, "Is that a new dress?"

"It was Shirley's," she says, meaning one of the married sisters, "but I added pleats and a lace collar."

"It looks nice," I offer.

"Thank you," she says, wary of my intentions.

Marylou says, "Have you heard from Adra?"

I remember how Marylou said Adra left because she got into trouble, but there is no trace of this in her voice now, so I answer, "She's in New Orleans and plans to go to college down there. She's working in a dress shop."

Marylou says, "I would love to work with clothes and keep up with all the newest fashions."

Lizzie says, "Marylou is good at designing clothes, as well as sewing."

"That's a real talent. I bet you could make a living doing something like that," I tell Marylou, meaning it. I am barely able to sew on buttons, much less design a dress.

"I don't know," Marylou says, "I'd have to leave Prosper, and I don't know how Mama could get along without me." Marylou gestures at her brothers and sisters, who are trying to climb a tree a little ways away.

"By the time you graduate, one of the others will be big enough to look after the smaller ones."

Marylou says, "I don't expect that day will ever come."

Lizzie says, "Cassie's right. Your sister Susan is ten. Start training her to take over for you."

It occurs to me that Marylou has something in common with Jan's sister, and so I say, "Jan's little sister Katia has stayed at home to help their mother while she was sick. She's going to be coming to school soon."

Marylou says, "At least I get to go to school. Mama doesn't go to work until I get home."

I knew Marylou's mother worked some to help the family, but I never thought how it affected Marylou. I never once thought about her at all. Her life is as foreign to mine as if she'd come from another country, and I've never tried to understand her.

Lizzie asks Marylou, "Do you know who that boy is, the one working with Jake and Jan?"

Marylou says, "His name's Amos Carter Brown. He's Sam Brown's cousin, come to stay with them. Sam didn't say, but I bet he got some girl in trouble."

That is so like Marylou to figure the worst.

Lizzie says, "Oh, I don't know. It might have been the other way entirely."

Later that afternoon the last log is placed, and there is a house standing. It seems incredible that in one day they can build a house that will last for years and years.

Later, when we are all eating fried chicken, I ask Jan about the new boy, the one Lizzie seems to like.

"He's very strong and works hard," Jan says.

Aunt Opal, who seems to like Jan, says, "So do you," and I am amazed, for it's a rare thing for her to say something nice. Mr. Mickey has gone around thanking everyone and especially Tom, who Mr. Mickey really likes. It seems as if everyone is feeling good about the day, and when the two Chance brothers get out their fiddles, Aunt Opal says, "I have been hearing from Cassie about how good you play. Go on over—they'll be glad to see you coming."

Jan turns to me and asks, "Will it be all right with you if I play with them for a while? Before we dance?" Jan already asked me to dance when we heard Tom tell about the square dance.

"Sure, I love to listen to you play." We walk over to where the fiddlers are tuning up.

Bill Chance sees us coming and says, "Get out that fiddle, boy. We sure do need all the help we can get."

They begin to play, and Jan listens, catching the tune before he joins them. They play the same tune one way and then change it a little, repeating the strain of music over and over, and it seems that one tune flows into another.

Bill Chance gets the people sitting around to stand up in squares and begins calling the dances. Daddy pulls Mama up, and they form a square with Tom and Lula, Jake and Nan, and Lizzie's mother and father. Lizzie has captured the new boy somehow and is holding his hand in one of the squares. Lizzie has never been known for shyness.

The caller gets people moving in a circle and then changing partners so that everyone dances with everyone else and never stops moving until the music stops. Then everyone rests a minute before the next round of dancing begins. I sit near Jan so I can watch him play and just feel the music around me.

Preacher Edwards and his wife have gone over to sit near Aunt Opal and Mr. Mickey. Bill Chance sees him sitting there and invites him to dance the next set. Says he's too young to be sitting with the old folks.

Only Preacher Edwards doesn't get up the way you'd expect, instead says he has a bad leg and has to pass. He says his wife might like to dance, but she refuses when the new boy Amos abandons Lizzie and walks over to ask her. He does not lack for daring, and I figure Lizzie is going to be in for trouble.

I watch Mama and Daddy dancing. As they dance, their expressions change, as if cares just fall away in the movement of the dance. After a while, Bill Chance says to Jan, "There's a pretty little girl been waiting for you to dance with her. Go on."

Jan packs his violin into the case and takes my hand. He says, "I was having such a good time playing, I almost forgot how much I wanted to dance with you. I cannot believe how lucky I am now to have you for my girlfriend."

I figure I am the lucky one, though, standing next to Jan, whose dark eyes catch the light from the lanterns. We join the circle where Lizzie is dancing again with the new boy. You don't have to know the dances to follow along. You just listen to the calls. We wind around a circle, changing partners and dancing with everyone. Sometimes you get lost and lose track of your partner, but then the caller sends you home to the place you began, and you wind up with your own partner. There is a pattern to the dance, and at the end you always wind up home. I wonder if there are patterns in life that you can follow if you could find them, only there's no one to call out directions. It sometimes seems you are all on your own. Well, not entirely, as I feel Jan catching hold of my hand. Thinking about being on my own makes me think of Adra all by herself in New Orleans. She's creating her own pattern for her life, but she's not entirely on her own either, for all of us think about her every day and pray she is all right. One day I know she will find her way back home.